"What is it..." Susan murmured, "that makes us speak to each other so suspiciously, with such doubt and question in our voices, or causes us to always be trying to explain away some innocent remark? Are you constantly on edge, or do I set you off?"

Thatch tightened his fists in his pockets. He could come up with several answers to Susan's questions. He was naturally suspicious, and she seemed naturally nosy. She was a member of the ship's staff, and he'd been sent undercover to investigate. He sighed. "I don't know, Susan. I think the problem is that I'm a private person and you always seem to be..."

"Prying?" she filled in for him. "I don't mean to, Thatch. I *like* people, I'm interested in them. If you have something to hide, that's your business. I'm not trying to find out anything you don't want to tell me."

He looked into her appealing brown eyes, and he wanted to confess everything he was thinking, everything he'd ever thought, everything he might think....

Dear Reader,

The summer is over, it's back to school and time to look forward to the delights of autumn—the changing leaves, the harvest, the special holidays . . . and those frosty nights curled up by the fire with a Silhouette Romance novel.

Silhouette Romance books always reflect the laughter, the tears, the sheer joy of falling in love. And this month is no exception as our heroines find the heroes of their dreams—from the boy next door to the handsome, mysterious stranger.

September continues our WRITTEN IN THE STARS series. Each month in 1991, we're proud to present a book that focuses on the hero—and his astrological sign. September features the strong, enticingly reserved Virgo man in Helen R. Myers's *Through My Eyes*.

I hope you enjoy this month's selection of stories, and in the months to come, watch for Silhouette Romance novels by your all-time favorites including Diana Palmer, Brittany Young, Annette Broadrick and many others.

We love to hear from our readers, and we'd love to hear from *you!*

Happy Reading,

Valerie Susan Hayward
Senior Editor

BRENDA TRENT

Dance Until Dawn

Silhouette *Romance*

Published by Silhouette Books New York

America's Publisher of Contemporary Romance

To J. F. Carroll, with deep appreciation for all you
did for T.K., and because I know you love cruises—
and Mexico!

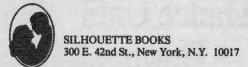

SILHOUETTE BOOKS
300 E. 42nd St., New York, N.Y. 10017

DANCE UNTIL DAWN

ISBN: 0-373-08816-7

First Silhouette Books printing September 1991

Books by Brenda Trent

Silhouette Romance

Rising Star #56
Winter Dreams #74
A Stranger's Wife #110
Run from Heartache #161
Runaway Wife #193
Steal Love Away #245
Hunter's Moon #266
Bewitched by Love #423
A Better Man #488
Hearts on Fire #506
Cupid's Error #540
Something Good #563
A Man of Her Own #620
Someone to Love #638
Be My Baby #667
A Woman's Touch #715
That Southern Man #757
For Heaven's Sake #778
Dance Until Dawn #816

Silhouette Desire

Without Regrets #122

Silhouette Special Edition

Stormy Affair #51

BRENDA TRENT

is the author of numerous novels and short stories. An inveterate traveler, she has visited most of the U.S. and much of the world, but confesses that the home in Virginia she shares with her pets is her favorite place. Her firm credo is that life is to be lived, and love is what makes it viable. Her passions include reading, movies, plays and concerts. But writing, she says, is her biggest passion and truly what makes all the rest of life meaningful.

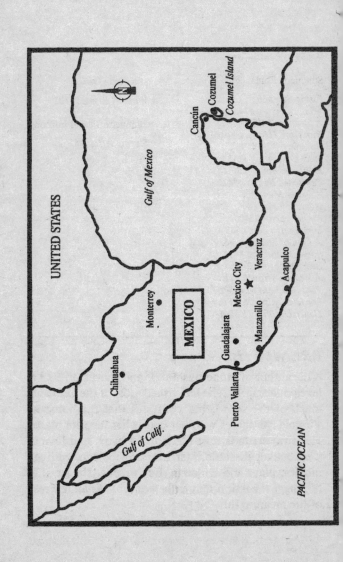

Chapter One

As Susan Williams tried to dodge a group of exuberant, excited and awed ship passengers, she murmured repeatedly, "Excuse me. Pardon me. Could I squeeze by, please?"

She couldn't have been running late at a worse time. After the trouble on the past few cruises, she knew management was uptight, even though supposedly the matter had been resolved.

It seemed to take forever to get through the crowd. Finally Susan headed toward the conference room, her long blond braid swaying against her back, her bangs dancing against her high forehead. She hardly noticed the man she passed in the hallway.

Seeing the blonde from the back—the position from which he spent most of his time observing people in his work as a private investigator—Thatch couldn't help but notice how shapely the woman was. He let his gaze

travel over her thick sun-lightened hair, down the
white blouse that covered her back, over her belted
slender waist, curvaceous hips in a sunny yellow skirt,
and lovely long legs, accented by the medium heels she
wore.

He decided if the front of her was at all comparable to the back, and if she was any indication of the
other females aboard ship, this job wasn't going to be
bad at all. In fact, he was looking forward to it. At the
very least, it would be easy on the eyes. Thatch moved
to catch up with the woman.

Susan sucked in her breath at the unexpected touch
of fingers on her arm.

"Ma'am. Excuse me. Ma'am?"

She turned, although she didn't have the time to
even pause. She was accustomed to being stopped by
passengers; she couldn't refuse the man a moment.

"Yes?" she asked a bit impatiently, unconsciously
staring at the large hand on her tanned skin.

The smile faded from the man's face as he withdrew his fingers. Susan looked into cool blue eyes and
wondered if her terse response had irritated him, or if
he was the type who was naturally tense.

Although the man was average-looking, about
thirty years old, maybe five feet ten inches tall, with an
athletic, wiry build, brown hair, and a rather ordinary full beard, there was something distinctive about
him. Susan couldn't put her finger on it at the moment, but, despite his fairly common features and the
casual way he was dressed, something set him apart.

Since she'd begun working on ships as a recreational assistant, she'd made it her business to study
people. Her first thought was that this man was too

defensive; too easily ruffled. But, then again, maybe that was why he was taking the cruise. Though people took cruises for a variety of reasons, she'd discovered most did so to forget their troubles for three weeks—especially on this particular cruise, the Christmas extravaganza.

But right now, she didn't have time to ponder this particular person's personality or problems.

"Can I help you with something?" she asked more pleasantly, her Southern drawl lilting, her smile dazzling. She was sorry she'd spoken sharply before. He couldn't know she was in a frantic hurry; the first day on ship was usually one of confusion for passengers. And he certainly couldn't know that she'd just spent a terrible time with her mother!

Thatch studied the woman as thoroughly from the front as he had from the rear. He wasn't disappointed. If anything, she was even more gorgeous than he had anticipated. The dramatic bright brown eyes, an unusual combination with the fair hair, made her exceptionally lovely. And she had dimples in her cheeks! Boy, was he a sucker for dimples! She intrigued him as no woman had done in a very long time.

Therein lay the rub. He was here to do a job, not become infatuated with a woman, especially a beautiful blond woman—with dimples *and* brown eyes!

During his eight years in this line of work, he'd been duped by clients and lied to by more than a few, yet the only one who'd ever left him scarred was a blonde much like this one. She wasn't the last, but none had wounded him as badly emotionally as she had.

It had taught him to avoid client-investigator involvement, and was a lesson he wasn't likely ever to forget. Even though he still had a penchant for blondes, he kept a healthy distance from ones as lovely as this.

"The Júbilo Deck?" he asked, having noted—albeit too late—the insignia on the woman's blouse, which indicated she worked on the ship. He'd thought all but the staff essential for boarding was assembled in the conference room.

His laconic question further convinced Susan that she'd either insulted him with her abrupt manner or he was one of those people who was naturally tense. Regardless, she didn't want to add to his unease.

"Take the elevator at the beginning of the hallway," she said. "Go up three decks."

She started to say he could get a map or ask for additional help at the registration desk, but he turned away abruptly without even a thank-you.

Susan resumed her rush down the hall, unconsciously thinking that it was ironic the man was housed on the Júbilo—the Spanish word for joy. Apparently whoever booked him on the cruise thought he could use some pleasure.

Shoving thoughts of the curt passenger aside, she went to the conference room and yanked the door open.

Thatch looked over his shoulder in time to see the blonde vanish. He found himself wondering if that syrupy Southern accent was affected. Abruptly he reminded himself to get his act together. He had a job to do, and he'd better be in the right frame of mind for it. He wouldn't learn anything by being hostile to the help. It was just that the woman . . .

He watched as the door closed, the image of her provocative figure and blond hair lingering behind. In his mind, he shifted through the ship's personnel files. He had reviewed them before his hasty assignment on this ship, but they were extensive and the blonde hadn't been nearly as dynamic or memorable in her picture as she was in person.

Smiling a little sourly, he told himself he would give her as wide a berth as possible. Still, he'd play the game as he'd been trained to play it, act out his role of first-time ship traveler until he solved the jewel thefts.

He grinned, thinking he sounded cocky; in truth, he *was* confident. If there was one thing he was good at, it was his job. Love wasn't his strong suit, he'd decided, so he concentrated on his career, which had paid off handsomely in monetary profits, respect in his field and satisfaction in a job well-done.

Sure, he'd failed some assignments for one reason or another, yet they were rare and the failure was usually beyond his control. He expected this job to be fairly easy.

He was supposed to be a passenger like any other, here for enjoyment, here to socialize. He could do that when he needed to. He could play the charmer or the cynic with equal ease, for life and people had taught him to be both.

Management had considered many covers for him, including hiring him as part of the help but finally decided he could mix with passengers *and* staff this way, without arousing anyone's suspicion.

However, he'd sure as hell better hide his cynical attitude and cool reaction to stunning blondes. He pulled his body up erectly, as if bracing himself. He wouldn't make such a mistake again.

Susan checked the time on the big clock on the conference-room wall. The ship, *Mexico Magic,* would sail shortly. Boarding was almost complete. She had missed the briefing the ship's owners insisted on before every sailing, despite this being the third trip this season.

"Susan, at last," Charles Masters said dryly, a frown on his tanned face.

The chastising expression in the recreational director's eyes embarrassed her. Susan knew he saw her failure to appear on time as a reflection on him. She loved her job; she owed a lot to Charles, who'd helped her get it.

At first, the owners had decreed her too young at twenty-five and too inexperienced to be of the greatest benefit to the varied group of people, including many elderly, who traveled on this particular ship. It was beside the point that Charles had possessed an ulterior motive; he'd still been the one to stress that she'd worked with the senior community in Charlottesville, Virginia, and had majored in physical education and recreational therapy at college.

Charles had sold her like a package, one that included genteel Southern upbringing, excellent manners, moneyed background and cultured demeanor, sure to appeal to people from another generation, a gentler generation. It had worked.

The only problem now was Charles himself, although it wasn't too hard to keep him at arm's length, for personal relationships between employees were discouraged. Their function on the extended cruise was to see to the guests' comfort and enjoyment.

"Please excuse my tardiness," Susan murmured, meeting Charles's eyes before her gaze encompassed the entire group in one apologetic sweep. "I missed my connection out of Atlanta," she added, her eyes fleetingly meeting the captain's, then the gazes of other employees, from the head housekeeper to the ship's doctor.

Susan had upset the system, a very delicate and expensive system where everyone was counted on to perform his or her best for people who paid thousands of dollars for three weeks of fun on the Christmas cruise to the Mexican Riviera.

"You're supposed to report in the night before, Susan," the captain said in a mildly rebuking voice.

"Captain," she responded, holding her heart-shaped chin a bit higher, "planes do get off schedule. There's quite a distance between Charlottesville, Virginia and Los Angeles, California, you know. I assure you I made every attempt to get here on time."

She'd been home to visit her mother who'd pleaded illness to coax Susan back. In truth, her mother had only wanted to resume the same battle she and Susan had fought since the younger woman refused to "give up that silliness of taking to the high seas as a hired hand."

Julia Williams was shamed by her daughter's literally sweating her time away as a recreational assistant, teaching aerobics classes, jogging and dancing about the ships' decks, "cavorting," as Julie referred to it, with total strangers.

Susan had been powdered, primped, prepped and pushed into the limelight from the time she was old enough to stand, dragged from high society to high society, with the specific purpose of making the right connection for marriage, becoming part of the right social network.

When her father died, removing the one buffer between her and her mother, Susan had ultimately fled to the farthermost safe harbor, or in this case, floating island, to escape Julia's charges that Susan was an ingrate, that she was throwing away her future, flouting all that Julia had done for her.

But Susan didn't want to be reminded of the painful arguments she and her mother had had over past history. Few people on the ship knew anything about Susan's background, and she intended to keep it that way. She usually said that she'd learned whatever good manners and so-called class she was supposed to have at school, which was partly true.

"The rest of us managed to get here on time," the captain said, interrupting Susan's reverie.

Keeping further excuses and explanations to herself, Susan nodded. She'd never been in trouble before. She was suddenly reminded of the stranger she'd met in the hall earlier. Perhaps it was best sometimes to keep silent.

When the captain, dressed in a smart brown-and-gold uniform, stood up, the other employees followed suit. "I'll leave you to be briefed by Charles," he told Susan. "Try to get to the meetings on time in the future."

Susan bit down on her full lower lip and forced herself not to take the reprimand too personally. "Yes, sir," she said.

The moment the others had filed out of the room to blend in with the general hubbub and excitement of imminent departure, Charles glowered at her, his blond crew cut and small slate-colored eyes making him look severe.

"You know this looks bad on me."

"Oh, Charles, really, I said I'm sorry. You know how manipulative Mother can be. She only wanted to throw another tantrum about my working."

"But you *are* working," he reminded her, "and 'I'm sorry' doesn't look impressive on your work record, or mine. Your mother will never approve of me if I don't make something of myself."

Tired and exasperated, Susan flung back, "Does it occur to you, Charles, that all the world doesn't revolve around your career or that it doesn't matter what my mother thinks of you? Why do you care?"

He stared at her for a moment, then said caustically, "The only way I know people like you and your mother is because I've been ambitious enough to pull myself up by my bootstraps. Some of us weren't born with a silver spoon in our mouth, Susan."

She sighed. "Well, Mother certainly wasn't, as I've told you, so I don't know why on earth you care what she thinks. I swear, sometimes you remind me of her. If a silver spoon is so important to you, you can have mine. You seem to want it badly enough."

His eyes glittered for a moment, then he caught her by the shoulders and drew her to him. "I don't want your silver spoon," he murmured. "I want you."

Susan desperately wished he wasn't renewing his pursuit. She was grateful to him, but she wasn't even slightly romantically interested. She had a definite kind of man in her mind and dreams, and Charles Masters wasn't the man. Nor was the string of rich, often titled men, young and old, Mother had insisted Susan meet. Before she could protest against Charles's advances, someone opened the door.

Thatch stared at the man embracing the woman, finding the pair intriguing. He'd known the room hadn't emptied completely; he'd stood in the shadows of the hall observing those leaving the meeting, matching each one up with the dossier he'd read. Because he'd been called in on the job at the last minute, his investigation of the staff had been hurried. He intended to rectify that at the first opportunity.

"Sorry," Thatch murmured, smiling sheepishly. Years of evasive tactics and thinking fast on his feet instinctively told him to play the fool. "I was told I might find the captain here—Hassler, I believe his name is. My travel agent said he'd arrange for the captain to give me a tour of the ship."

Charles faked a smile. "All the passengers will have the opportunity to tour the vessel at specifically designated times," he said, "but to my knowledge, no one on this cruise is guided personally by the captain, whose name, by the way, is Hassiter."

Susan, recognizing the man who'd asked for directions, didn't want him left with the impression that the staff was unfriendly. Charles was intentionally adding to the passenger's discomfort because he'd interrupted the romantic overture. She, on the other hand, was grateful for the intrusion.

"There's a schedule of all the activities and other pertinent information in your stateroom," she said, smiling warmly as she drew away from Charles. "Did you find your room all right?"

Appearing appropriately flustered, Thatch nodded. "The agent made it sound like he'd arranged something special with the captain just for me. He never mentioned that everyone takes the same tour."

Susan was good-naturedly empathetic. "Overeager travel agents say that all the time," she said, waving a hand dismissively. "We're used to it."

Thatch studied the blonde. She seemed genuinely willing to go out of her way to make him feel at ease. He didn't quite trust her interest in his welfare, yet he suspected she was sincere.

As Susan watched the man's expression change, his facial features relaxing, she vowed to see that he had a good time on the ship. His trip appeared to be starting out as unpleasantly as hers, and he'd paid money to have fun. Something told her having fun was difficult for him. She was beginning to suspect that the brusque manner he'd displayed previously was a cover for shyness.

"We're having two briefings for passengers in the Partido Room once we get under way," she said cheerfully. "It's done by meal seating schedule. Do you know which time you're slated for?"

Thatch shook his head. "I'm afraid I'm really out of my league here. I won this trip."

"That's great!" Susan exclaimed, with what Thatch considered a tad too much enthusiasm. "How did you win?"

He shrugged. "I work for an insurance company."
That wasn't exactly a lie. He frequently investigated
fraudulent insurance claims.

"And you were the most successful agent this
year?" Susan prompted, aware that many companies
gave free trips as incentives.

Thatch shook his head. "Not exactly. Just the most
persistent. I haven't been absent from work for eight
years." That wasn't a lie, either, though it wasn't the
truth in context.

"I see," she said. "How commendable!"

She should have guessed he wasn't aggressive
enough to win a competitive contest in the insurance
business, she told herself. At the moment, he reminded her of a bashful boy. He was decidedly refreshing after Charles, who had been practically
mauling her.

She held out her hand. "I'm Susan Williams, assistant recreational director."

Thatch found that he was mesmerized by dancing
brown eyes, a pretty smile and even white teeth. Her
hand was small, soft and tanned, her handshake warm
and friendly.

Thatch clasped her hand with more firmness than
he'd intended. Something about this woman's good
humor and attractive looks, her bubbling vivacity,
mesmerized him. For a moment they stared at each
other, then Charles spoke, shattering the hypnotic ef-
fect.

"Charles Masters," he said dryly. "I'm the recreational director."

"Oh, yes," Susan said, blushing slightly because
she'd been so enthralled by the other man she'd for-

gotten Charles was even there. "Excuse me. Charles is my boss."

Thatch was irritated by his attraction to the woman. He prided himself on being practical, and here he was nearly dizzy over this bright-eyed bundle of blond joy. She was, he told himself sourly, a little Miss Susy Sunshine if ever he'd seen one. He didn't know why he was fawning over her.

Giving his attention to the man, Thatch didn't extend his hand until Charles Masters did. His handshake was deliberately limp.

"Daniel Thatcher," he said.

"Charles and I are responsible for the social activities aboard ship," Susan said, reclaiming her positive attitude. For a moment, when the man was staring into her eyes, she'd completely lost her train of thought. She really must be tired!

"I'm afraid I'm not much for social affairs," he said. He stared out the porthole. "I'm not sure why I even came on the cruise. I'm really work-oriented," he continued distractedly.

That wasn't a lie. But of course he did have every intention of being social on board ship. He would need contacts to expose the jewelry thief.

"We'll have you mingling and mixing—and enjoying yourself in no time," Susan insisted happily. "I'm willing to bet you'll say you've had the time of your life when the cruise ends."

Thatch shrugged. He might at that. It was too early to tell. He couldn't seem to shake off his assessment of Susan Williams: vivacious and enthusiastic, the kind of woman who would do well in her position. She had a magnetic personality and a charming smile, not to mention the rest of her assets.

Thatch snapped back to attention. It was past time for him to leave when he started assessing a woman's attributes so favorably. She was, he firmly and cynically reminded himself, paid for such qualities and no doubt used her charm indiscriminately with all passengers. Whether she was sincere or not was a debate for another time.

"Thanks for the information." He glanced at Charles. "Sorry to have bothered you."

Charles managed a wan smile. "No bother. That's what we're here for—to see to passengers' comfort."

Thatch nodded, then turned to leave.

"Mr. Thatcher, you will be joining us at the briefing tonight, won't you?" Susan asked. "It's very informative and a good icebreaker."

He pretended reluctance, then spoke. "Yes." He waited until he reached the door before looking back at Susan. "By the way," he said, "my friends call me Thatch."

Her happy, contagious laughter drew Thatch's gaze to her full, parted pink lips. "Then I'll certainly call you Thatch, too! I do hope we're going to be friends."

Thatch opened the door and stepped outside without further comment. He couldn't afford to get caught up in this woman's charm and enthusiasm. He doubted if they would be friends. The business he was in discouraged friendships.

Susan Williams and Charles Masters, right along with everyone else aboard ship, were possible suspects. He never ruled out anyone until he was satisfied he or she wasn't culpable.

But, damn, he had to admit that he'd hate to find out that the vibrant beauty was involved in the crimes. Another time, another place—

He halted the reckless thought midway and headed back to his room to do some constructive thinking.

Chapter Two

Charles Masters watched the door close behind Thatcher.

"You don't honestly think he has any friends, do you? I suspect you're a minority of one calling him Thatch."

"Really, Charles," Susan said, annoyance creasing her pretty features. "I wish you wouldn't belittle people. I'm sure Thatch has his share of friends. If he doesn't, then he needs them. That's our job, remember?"

"No," he rebutted. "I'll baby-sit the passengers, but I don't intend to befriend them. I'm not paid *that* much. Anyhow, I wouldn't be that man's friend under any circumstances."

"You don't even know him!" she protested.

He sneered. "I know enough. He's a gullible fool. A travel agent told him the captain would give him a personal tour! Poor Hassiter wouldn't have time for anything except tours if he catered to hundreds of passengers' whims for individual attention."

"Thatch isn't the first one to fall for that line, and you know it," Susan defended. "Some travel agents promise the moon to a passenger, especially a hesitant one, which that man seems to be. Anyway," she added, "the captain isn't above a personal tour when a particular passenger warrants it."

"Ah, yes," Charles agreed, "but that passenger certainly isn't one of the chosen few. Management is giving away trips like crazy. I think it's time they put an end to it."

"Maybe they will now that Laurent has been fired."

Charles nodded pensively. "I hope that stops the thefts. Even though the items taken on the last two cruises were comparatively inexpensive and the owners were insured, that kind of thing is a disaster."

"How well I know," Susan murmured.

She'd been quite upset on the last cruise, as had everyone, when an elderly passenger's diamond necklace had been stolen from her cabin while she was at dinner.

"Ship security can only do so much! If the passengers would put that glitter and gold in the ship's safe, these things couldn't happen," Charles declared.

"That's true," Susan agreed, "but it's so inconvenient. They don't want to retrieve a piece of jewelry every time they decide to wear it."

"Then perhaps they deserve to be burglarized." Charles didn't wait for Susan's response. "It's amazing they know what they have, anyway, with so much razzle-dazzle strung over their bodies."

"Charles!" Susan exclaimed. "Your tirade is uncalled for."

She herself believed that money—or greed—was the root of much unhappiness, but there was no reason for Charles to condemn poor little old ladies who were trying to buy a small piece of pleasure, a tiny bit of attention, with their own money.

"It's not a tirade," he retorted. "I'm merely telling the facts. Women who flaunt their jewelry are asking for trouble. Many of those elderly ladies are lit up like neon signs, beckoning to burglars."

"Some of the poor dears have nothing except their money," Susan said passionately. "Their diamonds and gold are harmless vices they can well afford."

"You, of all people, would know about that, wouldn't you?" Charles muttered.

Susan was taken aback. "That's totally unjustified! I have never flaunted money. I've deliberately stayed away from that life, choosing to work, and I don't deserve your sharp tongue!"

"But, my dear," he said coldly, "*you* don't have to work at all, and that's the point, isn't it?"

"It is not!" she declared, feeling the same way she did when she battled with her mother. She clenched her fists in frustration. She worked because it filled a need in her, and Charles knew that!

"I don't see any point in continuing this conversation," she said, thinking she should leave before she said something she would regret. "If you want to brief me on the meeting, I'll listen. Otherwise, I'm going to my cabin."

Charles's eyes narrowed as he stared at Susan. He seemed poised to say something else tart, then abruptly he gained a semblance of control. Running his hands over his close-cropped hair, he drew a steadying breath.

"You're right," he agreed in a conciliatory tone. "I'm being envious and mean-spirited, aren't I? It's this business with the thefts."

"With Laurent gone, surely the stealing is a thing of the past," Susan soothed. "A random theft occurs on any ship, but the worst must be behind us on *Mexico Magic*."

"What if Laurent wasn't really the thief?" Charles asked. "After all, he was just a cabin boy."

"You caught him yourself!" Susan exclaimed.

Charles nodded. "Yes, I caught him with the goods, but what if he was just a front, a part of some kind of ring?"

"Oh, dear, I hadn't thought of that," Susan admitted, unconsciously stroking her long slim neck in a nervous gesture.

"It came up at the meeting," Charles said.

"Let's think positive," Susan stressed with more confidence than she felt. "Management has campaigned hard to offset word-of-mouth damage. They've slashed prices, advertised extensively, and we have a wonderful trip planned."

"Yes," Charles agreed. "However, cheap prices inevitably attract some undesirables. I hope we're not cutting off our noses to spite our faces with this strategy. After all, the owners are operating on a tight budget."

Reaching out to lightly touch his shoulder in an automatic gesture of concern, Susan said comfortingly, "I don't think you have to worry, Charles. You can get a job anywhere, even if *Magic* goes under." She didn't confide in him how devastated she would be if that happened. *Magic* had become her home, her refuge.

Charles tightly clasped her hand before she could move it. "I'm going to share a secret with you, Susan. I've invested money in *Magic*. If Roarr & Company goes under, so do I."

"I didn't know they were offering stock," she said, freeing her hand from his grasp.

"It's not general knowledge, so don't repeat it," he said. "The company solicited only a few select investors to help stabilize the situation. That's why it's urgent the bad press be stopped."

"Our first priority is the passengers," Susan stressed. "The thefts must be stopped so people can feel safe."

"One follows the other," he said logically. "Of course I'm concerned about the passengers, but I'm concerned about the company, too. Not just for myself, you understand, but also for the rest of the investors."

"I believe everything is going to be all right," Susan persisted. "If Laurent was the thief, we're worrying needlessly." She smiled. "Now, if you're through with me, I want to catch a quick nap before the passenger briefings."

Charles put his hands on her small waist. "I'm not through with you . . ."

Prying his fingers free, Susan pleaded, "Charles, give up! You talk about worrying about your job. You know management discourages fraternizing between employees."

"That rule isn't meant for the upper-echelon employees," he said dryly. "You know it's for the little—"

"It's for *all* of us," she interrupted. "And aside from rules, I've explained I want only your friendship. I don't want to hurt your feelings, but I'm not interested in a romantic relationship."

"Why must you be so stubborn?" he demanded. "We're perfect for each other. Where else will you find another man who'll be supportive of your career, indeed one who shares it! Why can't you be reasonable and see that I'm the man for you, Susan?"

"I don't love you, Charles," she said simply.

"You will," he insisted. "Just give us a chance."

She sighed, thinking how utterly impossible he was today. There was no point in arguing with him. "Charles, it's not going to happen. Period. Now, if you'll excuse me..."

Trembling a little inside from frustration and exhaustion, she walked out of the room and firmly shut the door behind her. Fortunately the ship would be under way soon and Charles would be occupied with his duties.

She hoped the group was homogeneous. The last thing she needed was a ship full of people who didn't want to get to know each other. It made all of her and Charles's efforts to plan events so much harder.

A picture of the passenger called Thatch surged into Susan's mind. She was surprised by the nagging notion that she involve him in the ship's abundant activities. Sometimes a person wanted to be left alone while aboard. Susan understood that isolation was thera-

peutic for some, yet she was determined to have
Thatch take part in the festivities on the ship.

But was she more interested in his welfare, or her
own? He had captured her attention. She wanted to
get to know him. She wasn't really sure why. The
thought troubled her.

Charles had made a relevant point: it was difficult
to meet a man compatible with her career. Her former boyfriend had quickly become disenchanted when
Susan began working on the ship. He'd said he wasn't
about to marry a career sailor, which she supposed she
was.

A vision of Thatch tugged at the edges of her mind.
Susan suspected if the right man came along—the *real*
right man, not someone her mother tried to thrust off
on her...

She shoved the thought aside. The fact of the matter was that it wasn't wise to focus on a given passenger, especially an appealing man who would disappear
from her life as quickly as he had appeared.

In his cabin, Thatch removed his shoes and
stretched out on the bed. The room was small yet
comfortable and colorfully decorated. He'd purposely been put in medium-priced accommodations so
that he would be more acceptable to both the rich and
the not-so-rich.

As he lay there, his mind churning furiously, he
mentally reviewed the personnel files. The image of
Susan Williams in Charles Masters's arms popped into
his mind.

He shuffled past the picture, recalling instead Laurent, the Frenchman who'd ostensibly been the thief.

Management was convinced he'd been framed, that the necklace had been planted.

But by whom? The arrow didn't always point in the proper direction in this business; the seemingly obvious wasn't necessarily the truth. In his years as a private investigator, Thatch had learned that anyone could be the culprit.

Management strongly suspected someone on the staff was guilty, and Laurent had agreed to go along with the plan, temporarily giving up his job. The idea was to get the real thief to drop his guard, make him feel secure enough to become careless, thereby making him easier to catch.

Thatch knew a repeat passenger could be responsible, although he leaned toward management's belief that it was an employee. He'd gotten a brief rundown on both passengers and employees before boarding. The knowledge that there were several repeat passengers complicated matters.

It had amazed him that someone would take the same trip on the same ship again and again until he'd learned that most of the repeat passengers were the aging rich with time and money to spare. They felt more comfortable with a routine they knew and people who knew them from previous trips.

Many of them traveled continuously, going from place to place, not really caring about their destination. However, they did care about their safety, their property, their sense of well-being.

Tensing at the unexpected knock on his door, Thatch forced himself to slow down mentally as he went to answer.

He hadn't really known whom to expect, a cabin boy perhaps, but Susan Williams's sudden appearance unsettled him as much as it had the first time he'd seen her.

In spite of all his training and his efforts to appear at ease, he felt stiff from the tips of his toes to the top of his head, as though he'd encountered a physical threat. The reaction disturbed him; he'd developed almost a sixth sense in his years in the business and had an instinctive awareness of danger. Still, he felt ridiculous being so uncomfortable with this woman.

"So, you did find your room all right," she said animatedly, despite sensing that Thatch wasn't pleased to see her.

He nodded, then cleared his throat before speaking, unsure he could deal with Susan. Although he often encountered the unexpected, she was one surprise he couldn't seem to handle.

"Yes." The monosyllable was terse.

Susan could feel her face turning red, but she pressed on. "I didn't know if you'd located the information I mentioned or not. I thought I'd stop by before going to my cabin to make sure you knew which meal seating you had."

Thatch smiled faintly. He didn't want this particular woman's personal attention, though to be practical, he supposed he should welcome it. She might prove invaluable—if he could manage to think coherently when he saw her.

Resolving to get past whatever bothered him about Susan Williams, Thatch scrutinized her. He was struck by the fact that she really wasn't like any blonde he'd

ever met, no matter how determined he was to cate-
gorize her.

This blonde was a shapely, extroverted working
woman, a walking testimonial to healthy sea air, ship
activities and interaction with people.

If she was anything like she presented herself, she
was warm, open and interested in others, as well as
interesting herself. She possessed an indefinable self-
possession that spoke of confidence—no, class! That's
what it was. He was surprised to see the characteristic
in the assistant recreational director.

Hell! Thatch thought, listening to the accolades he
was heaping on Susan, she was packaged for the trip!
He tried to dredge up everything he could about her
from the files; but to his chagrin, for he was desperately trying to discredit her for his own protection, his
mind drew a blank.

When Thatch didn't comment, Susan looked away.
Clearly, engaging him in the ship's social agenda was
going to be like pulling teeth. The man resented her
personally, or he was tongue-tied. Either way, he was
difficult to talk with and she found herself chattering
inanely.

"If I could just step inside, I could check the
schedule myself and tell you what time your seatings
are. I didn't bring a timetable with me and I don't
know the division line. It breaks up here on the Júbilo Deck, though I'm not sure which room."

Thatch didn't want her to come in. He hadn't yet
decided where to stow his personal effects. Without a
word, he moved away, grabbed the schedule from the
desk and thrust it at her.

"I must say this is a personal touch I didn't anticipate," he murmured, critically examining her expression. "Are all passengers treated so well, or am I being
singled out?"

He'd seen pushy women before, and this one seemed
to be bending over backward to accommodate him.
He wondered why. Susan Williams naturally set off his
suspicious nature.

Still, he hadn't meant to ask her quite like that, totally without tact. Because he'd learned that a bad
choice of words didn't sound any better when one tried
to correct it, he let the question hang between them.

Susan's fingers were shaking slightly as she took the
schedule. He *had* been singled out; there was no point
in telling herself that it was no more than what she'd
do for any other passenger who seemed uncomfortable and apt not to enjoy the cruise. She wished she
hadn't come here, yet she was drawn to the man, as if
pulled by a magnet.

Giving him an unsteady smile, she said, "I'm hired
to see to the comfort of all the passengers, Mr.
Thatcher. I felt that we got off on the wrong foot when
you asked for help in locating your room. I was in a
hurry. Still, that was no reason for curtness. In fact,"
she said pointedly, resenting the uncomfortable way he
made her feel and wanting to crack his cool facade,
"there is no excuse for rudeness on anyone's part."

Thatch realized that they were headed farther in the
wrong direction, which was bad manners *and* bad
business on his part. Susan Williams bemused him.
She seemed sincere, guileless and dedicated, but that
was part of her job. She, like he, had learned to work
with people, to anticipate, to...

He paused. Perhaps he was basing her job on his own, and that definitely wasn't only unfair, it was also unrealistic. In his work, he had encountered more than his share of unsavory characters. His suspicions were deeply ingrained and learned the hard way, while he'd put himself at risk.

There was no reason to believe that this woman was anything other than what she appeared.

At least until she proved herself otherwise.

"I agree," he said.

He stepped outside the room, standing beside Susan, trying to see the schedule she was gripping so tightly. Her nearness made him more acutely aware of her beauty and more wary of her personal interest. He wasn't oblivious to the fact that he was only average in looks—interestingly average, he added, his ego coming to the forefront, but definitely not a standout in a crowd.

That was something that worked to his advantage on the job, though suddenly he wished that he was this woman's consuming concern and that he really was on vacation, meeting her purely for fun.

However, that wasn't the case.

"When do I eat?" he asked.

Susan stared at the schedule listing the three-week itinerary. It seemed overwhelming at first, although a close examination revealed it was well thought out and easy to follow day-by-day. The initial page broke down special occasions that separated the decks by time and date.

"Here," she said, pointing. "You have the first seating. Six-thirty. Júbilo Deck, rooms one through one hundred."

She looked at him, noting again that he wasn't much taller than she was, yet he seemed to have great presence. Her reasonably good assessment of people abandoned her in this man's case. Here, alone with Thatch, women's intuition told her that he wasn't the bashful boy she'd believed him to be when he'd interrupted her and Charles.

As she'd thought earlier, there was an edge to him, mentally and physically. Every lean line was honed and defined. She'd worked with enough men in the exercise classes to know that this one took excellent care of his body, but that wasn't all. There was an ... *alertness,* for lack of a better word, about him.

Realizing she was staring, she looked away from his penetrating blue eyes. Maybe she was just intimidated because of his alertness. His Jekyll-and-Hyde behavior confused her. As though hypnotized, she found her gaze returning to those eyes, but she was still uncertain of whether he appreciated her presence.

When their gazes locked, Susan felt the erratic beating of her heart, felt the pounding of her pulse at her throat, and wondered if her legs were going to support her. She'd never experienced anything comparable to her heated awareness of this man or her vulnerability to his maleness. It frightened her!

Thatch's gaze shifted lower, scanning Susan's small, attractive nose, full lips and heart-shaped face. Something about her set off an unexpected yearning inside him. He had a compelling urge to trace her face with his thumb, to see if that smooth tanned skin was as silky to the touch as it looked. His fingers ached to satisfy the desire to connect with her in some intimate way.

Wondering what the hell was happening to him, Thatch catapulted himself out of his swirling sensual fantasies before he could act on them. He was a grown man, for crying out loud, not some adolescent mooning over his first pretty girl!

"Thank you, Miss Williams. I hope I'll see you at the briefing." When he spoke, he shattered the tension and diffused some of the electricity that was so strong he believed he could almost be shocked by it.

His manner was pleasant, but his disturbing gaze never left hers. Susan automatically corrected him on the use of her surname, glad for something sensible to say after the draining experience of being drawn into the depths of Thatch's blue eyes.

"Please call me Susan. We don't stand on formality here on the ship."

"No?" He raised heavy brows. "I thought I heard you call me Mr. Thatcher. Pity, too," he mused. "I explained that my friends call me Thatch."

Susan braced herself for more of the unexpected with this man. He had her running mentally around in circles. She had called him Mr. Thatcher, as was usual to show respect to the passengers, but that had been when she thought he resented her. Of course she recalled his request that she call him Thatch; it just hadn't seemed that they were going to be friendly.

"I do want to call you Thatch," she murmured, "if you think we can be friends."

He nodded, for a moment believing the lie himself, though he knew the chances were doubtful under the circumstances.

"I hope so," he said.

Susan made herself break eye contact with him. "Good." She tried to sound casual, in spite of the giddy way she felt. "I'll see you at six-thirty."

"Yes," he agreed. His voice softened a bit. "Thanks for coming, Susan."

"No trouble," she said, backing away from his door, unavoidably glancing at him again. He was smiling, his lips parting to reveal very white teeth in contrast to the darkness of his beard.

He took a couple of steps forward and held out his hand. "My schedule."

Susan found herself giggling like a nervous schoolgirl. "Sorry," she said, handing it back to him. Then she turned and fled.

Thatch watched her go, thinking again what a shame it was he was here on business. Spy business! Susan Williams stirred something inside him, something dormant that he'd thought he'd never feel again, something oddly hopeful. He didn't understand it, he didn't like it, but he was looking forward to seeing her. That definitely wasn't smart!

Susan risked a quick look over her shoulder as she headed around the corner toward the elevator. Thatch was watching her, pensively pulling on his beard. She rushed on, wishing she knew what it was about the man that entranced her.

Suddenly she shivered. She'd witnessed more than her share of shipboard romances, although she'd never had one. They usually lasted for the duration of the trip, and somebody either took home a lot of warm, fond memories, or a broken heart.

She didn't want either. When she found the man of her dreams, she wanted to take him home. Forever.

Anxiously she pressed the elevator button. If she didn't hurry, she wouldn't have time for a nap at all, and God knew she needed one.

Chapter Three

After donning a flowered shirt, white slacks and blue deck shoes, Thatch checked his appearance in the mirror a final time before going to the passenger briefing. He'd worn many disguises in his line of work. While this one wasn't the worst by any stretch of the imagination, the bright blue flowered shirt, coupled with the unfamiliar feel of the beard, made him feel silly. He hadn't known what an actor he would have to be when he'd decided to become a private investigator. He'd soon learned that he was selling himself first, then his skills, whether it was to client or suspect.

He shoved his personal effects and his room key into his pocket and left. It was time to get to work.

"Thaddeus Waller? Thaddeus, is that you behind the beard?"

Thatch cringed inwardly as his eyes met those of the woman coming toward him. *Caught!* echoed through his mind. He experienced a sinking sensation in his stomach as he continued down the hall, deliberately pretending not to be Thaddeus Waller, one of his more inventive, memorable aliases.

Obviously he wasn't as well disguised as he'd thought—always a danger to any man trying to go undercover yet maintain some semblance of his own identity in case he was put on the line.

"Thaddeus?"

In spite of picking up his pace, he wasn't fast enough to escape the woman. As they passed, he felt, then saw, a long-nailed hand on his arm.

He faced her. "I beg your pardon?"

She studied his face carefully. "Sorry. I thought you were—well, never mind who. Just someone else."

Thatch let his gaze trail over the buxom bleached blonde. He wouldn't have recognized her if he'd seen her photo, and obviously he hadn't noted her name on the long list of passengers when he'd scanned it. It simply wasn't possible to avoid everyone from his past.

But now, with her standing right in front of him, he did recognize the woman. She'd been a redhead when he'd last seen her. Merry Lou Granger, New York City, four years ago, premarital investigation. Her wealthy fiancé had suspected her motives for marriage of being monetary.

Thatch had passed himself off as Thaddeus Waller, a wealthier suitor than her fiancé. Merry Lou had merrily and quickly taken the bait without giving a thought to her two-karat engagement ring. Fortunately the fake pursuit had lasted only three weeks before she agreed to be Thaddeus Waller's bride. Then

Thatch hastily bowed out, pretending to be heartbroken upon discovering Merry Lou was already engaged to another man.

"No problem," Thatch said.

He nodded brusquely, then continued on his way. To his irritation, Merry Lou Granger wasn't about to be put off so easily, whether she thought she knew him or not.

"Are you travelling alone?" she asked, catching up with him. "I am." She laughed. "I'm on a divorce recovery cruise, having finally shed my husband without losing everything else, including my proverbial shirt." She extended that long-nailed hand. "Merry Lou Addison."

So, Thatch thought, she'd apparently managed to marry some guy named Addison, no doubt with a ton of money and he'd no doubt caught on to her scheme *after* the ceremony.

It was people like Merry Lou, both male and female, who'd convinced Thatch that marriage could be an *un*holy state. For more reasons than one, he definitely didn't want to encourage this woman, yet by the same token, he didn't want to be overtly rude.

"Nice to meet you," he said, not revealing his name.

"And you?" she prodded. "Who are you?"

This was an awkward situation. Although Thatch suspected Merry Lou couldn't be sure he wasn't who he said he was, "Thatch" was too close to "Thaddeus" to leave him feeling comfortable. This could really cause trouble.

When he didn't answer her question immediately, she laughed again. "Excuse my boldness. A woman alone has to watch out for herself. I hope you won't think me too forward if I say I'm not sorry I mistook you for someone else. I like men with beards and blue eyes. You are single, aren't you?''

Thatch shoved his hands into his pockets, determined to offer as little information as possible. ''I'm flattered, but if you'll excuse me, my single state is due to a natural disaster.''

Another slightly askew tale, although his experience with blondes, of which Merry Lou was now one, could be considered a natural disaster, creating havoc in the heart and head. He didn't need or want damage to his wallet, too, with a woman like this one.

Apparently not a person to be put off, and still not satisfied, Merry Lou scrutinized Thatch more carefully. He had no choice but to be blunt, for fear she might think she knew him, after all.

''I prefer to be alone,'' he murmured.

''Oh!'' she said, clearly surprised, yet still searching his face.

Thatch strode off, wondering about the wisdom of using a shortened version of his real name, Daniel Thatcher Thomas, for this job. He let the air escape from his lungs in a long sigh, then told himself he would simply have to hope he'd halted Merry Lou in her tracks and make the best of whatever else might happen.

''Thatch! Over here!''

He drew in his breath, wondering who else had discovered him, until he saw Susan Williams. He didn't know how far behind him Merry Lou was and he dared to look back. Good, she'd vanished into the crowd.

Thatch headed in Susan's direction. He had to hand it to the woman: she was hell-bent on helping him enjoy the cruise and from the looks of her this evening, that wouldn't be hard to do.

Dressed in canary-yellow cropped pants, a brief yellow-and-white halter top that exposed a hint of creamy cleavage, a matching blouse and yellow sandals that wrapped around her slender ankles and drew attention to her long legs, she was picture pretty. Her blond hair cascaded in loose waves about her shoulders like a fluffy, golden cloud.

"Why don't you sit here with Charles and me?" Susan offered warmly, indicating a chair. "I'm glad you decided to come."

The woman seemed so sincere that Thatch found himself wanting to believe her. It was very difficult for him not to be flattered. She was the most appealing woman he'd encountered in years.

He found himself thinking of her in foolishly sentimental phrases: she was like a single long-stemmed buttercup in all that yellow; her delicate scent was like wildflowers on a spring evening; the combination, with her full, well-defined figure, reminded him of a lush bouquet of yellow roses.

Thatch didn't realize he was still standing, staring at Susan, until she patted the chair beside her as if she were coaxing a child. "Here."

"Thanks," he managed. "I'm sure I'll find the information useful."

Ignoring Charles's brooding expression, Thatch settled down uncomfortably on the other side of Susan. She must think him an idiot; his encounters with her had been awkward, to say the least. He tried not to look at her again, but she wasn't as easy to ignore as Charles was.

All Thatch's senses were heightened by her nearness; his entire system sped up. He really didn't understand this lack of control. He was schooled in dealing with people after eight years of being a private eye, handling clients of every kind with every conceivable problem and expectation, yet this was something new for him.

He'd known about physical attraction as long as he'd known there were pretty women in the world, but this was an overpowering awareness that was unwarranted, unwise and unwelcome, considering the situation. He wasn't in control here, and that left him feeling out of kilter.

He wanted to blame it on the unfamiliar motion of the ship, but he knew better. There was no denying that this woman drew him like a divining rod to water. He *felt* like a divining rod; he was vibrating all over!

All of his survival instincts warned him to keep a discreet distance, yet common sense told him that wasn't smart. He knew Susan Williams might prove useful to his investigation.

Thatch frowned. He didn't want to 'use' Susan in his investigation, no matter how advantageous the alliance.

What he really wanted to do was court her here amid the glamorous atmosphere of the cruise ship. The setting was ripe for wooing, the woman was a dream, and she was going out of her way to cater to him, no matter how much she denied it.

What more could one man want?

Thatch interlocked his fingers and clasped them tightly, struggling against the absurd desire to put his arm around the back of Susan's chair and get a little closer. *The job,* he reminded himself sternly, pressing his palms together. He had to concentrate on the job; that meant he was going to have to discourage Susan Williams's interest.

More to the point, he was going to have to put the brakes on *his* interest in her! It was simply too risky. In fact, it was downright ridiculous.

How could he conduct a covert operation with her on his mind? How could he survey the other crew members and passengers who numbered in the hundreds and come up with the culprit if he was besotted with this blonde?

Already the job was like looking for a needle in a haystack. In the past he'd seen such a quest as a challenge, a conquerable puzzle that tested his physical and mental strength, that put him on a par with ancient warriors fighting the forces, although he was making conquests in the concrete jungle of modern society.

Hell, he told himself, he *sounded* like an idiot! He'd never been prone to sentimentality or fantasy—well, at least not for a long, long time, not since he'd become experienced on the job. Once he'd walked on the wild side of life, he'd seen the world differently.

Now all he saw was the woman beside him. He'd never known himself to be this weak-kneed, waxing poetic, a mess of mixed emotions over a woman he didn't even know.

When Susan glanced at Thatch, she was disappointed to see how stiffly he sat, as if he didn't want to be there. Maybe he *didn't,* she told herself despairingly, the thought depressing her way out of proportion to the situation. She didn't even know the man, for heaven's sake!

But, goodness, she was determined to. Her desire bordered on obsession. It was absurd. She'd met hundreds of appealing men aboard ship, and this had never happened before.

She sighed when Jason, the ship's spokesman, took the microphone in hand and began to make general announcements about emergency procedures, then more pleasant topics. Susan had heard it all before, but even if she hadn't she couldn't concentrate.

What was it Thatch didn't approve of? Was it her? Or was it himself he was displeased with? And why did it matter so much?

She'd seen troubled passengers before and she prided herself on getting them to relax, to make the most of their time on board. This man, though, was different.

She was acutely aware that he sat rigidly at her side, appearing to want to keep distance between them at all costs. He made *her* ill at ease. She felt rejected.

A new and disturbing thought filled her mind. What she really wanted was for him to take an interest in her! That was dreadful. She'd already reminded herself of the futility of shipboard romances.

When she heard Jason say her name, she started. Quickly forcing a smile to her lips, she went with Charles to the front of the room. As she and Charles talked about the activities they had planned, Susan scanned the assembly.

The huge room was filled with the chatter of excited passengers who barely calmed down enough to listen to the details of excursions to be taken at Puerto Vallarta, Manzanillo, Acapulco, Ixtapa/Zihuatanejo, Mazatlan and Cabo San Lucas, and the lineup of events taking place aboard ship along the way.

Susan spied the empty chair beside the one she'd been sitting in. Thatch had left! When she'd finished her talk, she walked out of the hall, too, much to Charles's surprise.

"Where are you going, Susan?" he demanded, hurrying after her. "You have to stay for the second seating assembly, and the question-and-answer sessions."

Susan pressed her fingers to her temples, trying to stop the throbbing that signaled a headache. "You do it, Charles. You're the director, and you know everything I have scheduled."

"Why can't you?" he asked, the familiar frown lining his forehead. "It's *your* job!"

Susan sighed. "I'm too tired and I've got a headache. I'm sorry. I promise I'll make it up to you."

Charles studied her face for a moment. "All right, but I mean to hold you to that promise," he said tightly.

Only half listening, Susan nodded and turned away. What she needed was a glass of wine to soothe her nerves and make her forget her preoccupation with Thatch.

A thousand thoughts were tumbling about in her head by the time she reached the lounge. And there, sitting at a stool at the bar, was the focus of them all.

Thatch turned around as Susan paused at the entrance, almost as if he sensed her presence.

Susan stroked her neck, causing slight red marks. The man must think she was dogging him, and that wasn't true. At least not this time. She really had savored the thought of a quiet moment to herself to prepare for sleep. She'd been too tired when she'd tried to nap earlier. She suspected that was a preview of the coming night.

For a moment she vacillated, not knowing whether to walk away or force a smile and say how surprised she was to see Thatch. There were other lounges where she could get a glass of wine.

Watching her, Thatch alternated between rising irritation and feeling flattered. He'd tracked enough people in his career to know when someone was determined not to let up. And this woman was determined! It occurred to him that, just as Merry Lou Addison had discovered who he was, perhaps so had Susan Williams.

He smiled to himself. He was getting paranoid. Why would she even want to discover who he was? He'd never seen this woman in his life, and she'd never seen him. Surely she was in the bar by coincidence. She'd been talking when he left the meeting. Unless she had psychic powers, he seriously doubted that she could have known his destination.

With several lounges on board, he hadn't known himself where to go. As he had, Susan had probably picked this one because it was close to the Partido Room. In reality he was behaving foolishly, calling unnecessary attention to himself by trying to avoid her.

Before Susan could make up her mind what to do, Thatch solved the problem for her.

"Hello, Susan. I didn't expect to see you here."

"Nor I you," she said, clearly flustered. "I dropped by for a quick glass of wine to help me unwind a bit. All the rushing about and hype of the first night at sea..." she said, letting her voice trail away.

Thatch's smile was slow and lazy. "You know the old saying about great minds thinking alike," he murmured. "Come join me for a drink." He indicated the stool beside him.

As Susan moved nearer, she didn't know why she felt so uneasy. She'd vowed she was going to spend some time with Thatch. This almost empty room couldn't be a more perfect place if she'd planned it.

Or could it?

She was acutely aware that the man was revealing that he had a sort of Jekyll-and-Hyde personality again. He hadn't seemed at all comfortable sitting beside her in the group room. In fact, she remembered her feelings of rejection because he'd seemed so ill at ease with her.

Now he was smiling, inviting her to join him. What did it mean? What *could* it mean?

Shoving aside the bothersome and useless questions, Susan made herself deal with the moment. Thatch was here and she was here. They'd share a little time and a drink. Period.

"So, what do you think of the social events planned?" she asked eagerly as she climbed onto the stool beside him.

His gaze automatically strayed to her long legs as she seated herself. If he'd ever seen a typical all-American blond beauty, Susan Williams was it.

Shifting his thoughts to her question, he looked down at his beer as he ran his thumb through the moisture on the outside of the mug. "This is all new to me," he said. "I'm not sure I'm going to like being on a ship."

"I wish you wouldn't say that!" she exclaimed. "You simply don't know how much fun you're going to have. This is a great way to travel. You don't have to drag your luggage all over, constantly rummaging around in it for items. Everything's right there in your room. You can have all the comforts of home—more for many people—and still go places."

Thatch noticed the way she gestured with her hands, her sexy Southern drawl, her animated face. Miss Susy Sunshine, he thought to himself again, blond, upbeat, bright and beautiful. But this time he grinned.

"All right. I believe you. You do a better job of selling than a travel agent," he teased.

Susan was ready to protest when she saw his blue eyes twinkling. She laughed. In truth, she had been selling.

"Sorry," she said. "I simply love ship travel so much that I want all the passengers to have a good time. It's difficult for some of them, especially shy singles."

He bent over his beer a little further, then took a long drink. His eyes lost their glow when they met her bright brown ones.

"Is that what you think I am? A shy single?"

Susan's face turned red. What was he trying to tell her? Or *not* tell her? That he wasn't shy? Or that he wasn't single? What on earth prompted her to think he was single just because he was alone? He wasn't the first man to travel without his wife.

"I don't know," she answered. "Are you?"

The frank question made Thatch want to answer her truthfully. *That* thought brought his scattered senses under control. He'd been flirting with Susan and enjoying it. But that wasn't why he was here.

He studied his mug of beer. "I suppose that's an accurate description." At least sometimes, he wanted to add. Like now, when the guise worked well. Or maybe all the time.

He was taken aback by the thought. He *was* single, and the job had made him withdraw.

He tensed when he felt Susan's touch on his shoulder. It was an automatic reaction to an approach by a stranger, a trained response, startling him from his thoughts, putting him on the alert.

Seeing his discomfort, Susan quickly withdrew her hand. "I'm sorry," she murmured. "It's easy for me to forget that some people don't like to be touched, particularly by someone they don't know."

Thatch met her sympathetic brown eyes, then quickly looked away. He couldn't think of anything at the moment that he'd like more than her touch. He certainly didn't want her sympathy; however, she was building a definite profile of him in her mind, and instinct told him to go with it until he knew her better.

"I've been hitting some rough times lately," he said, offering another of his ambiguous truths. "I'm a little jumpy."

Susan was willing to accept any excuse other than that he didn't want her here. "I'll say. And I seem to bring out the worst in you, when really all I'm trying to do is help you relax."

He smiled at the irony. He couldn't relax around this woman, regardless of circumstances. Even if he didn't have to keep the job paramount in his mind, her nearness unsettled him in the primitive way certain women had disturbed men since the beginning of time. She was too damned sensual to ignore and he was in no position to do anything about it.

He watched as the bartender brought Susan a glass of white wine. "Now, that's what I call service," he said, grateful for a change in subject. "You didn't even have to order."

She smiled. "Dennis and I have worked on this ship the last three trips. He knows the only thing I ever drink is white wine."

The bartender went away as silently as he'd arrived. Thatch found himself studying the man, flipping through the files in his mind, assessing Dennis as a possible thief. A bartender would have plenty of opportunities to get to know lonely older women. Thatch knew how glib barkeeps generally were. Some people talked as openly with them as they did with their doctors.

"He's a nice man," Susan said.

Thatch stared at her, wondering if she'd read his mind.

"Dennis," she said, indicating the bartender. "He's easy to talk to and the passengers seem to like him." She smiled again. "Well, most of them," she amended. "Sometimes we get people on board who don't like anybody, themselves included. They're very difficult to please, no matter how much the staff tries.''

Thatch asked himself if the woman was analyzing him, putting him in the category of those who didn't like anyone. He had a compelling need to assure her that wasn't the case.

''Often it just appears that people are being difficult,'' he murmured. ''I've learned that there are times, situations, in everyone's life when they have to take a breather, step back and go into themselves for a while. I should think you'd get your share of those people on a ship, people seeking isolation, knowing no one can reach them here on the ocean.''

''Is that what you're doing, Thatch?'' Susan asked boldly, driven to know something concrete about this enigmatic and evasive man.

Thatch chuckled. This woman would make a wonderful private investigator. He got most of his best answers by putting questions to people bluntly, catching them off guard. There was something about an unexpected question that brought out spontaneous truths.

The trick was not to be the person doing the confessing, which was achieved by putting the other person on the defensive. Thatch quickly tried the theory on Susan.

''Tell me, why are you so interested in my life?'' he asked.

The blush that crept up Susan's neck was so crimson it was visible in the muted light of the lounge. She honestly didn't know why she was subjecting herself to this man. She was weary enough this evening without adding to it.

"Sorry," she said tightly. "I truly am not trying to be nosy. My only intention was friendliness."

When he saw the way Susan stiffened her spine and clasped her wineglass with both hands, Thatch immediately regretted his handling of the situation. He'd put her on the defensive all right, and now he was ashamed.

"I'm the one who's sorry," he apologized.

Susan didn't look at him, but Thatch continued to gaze at her, seeking to uncover clues to why she was so set on getting to know him. When he saw her hands tremble as she lifted her glass to her mouth, he felt like an ogre. She was putting him in a back-against-the-wall position, and he needed to cope with it better than he was doing.

"I think you implied earlier that there was no excuse for rudeness, so I won't offer one," he added. "Perhaps after eight years of constant work, I don't know how to enjoy myself with a beautiful woman who's going out of her way to be nice. I don't deserve your attention."

Susan kept her eyes lowered, her long lashes shadowy against her classic cheekbones. She didn't want Thatch to see her dismay.

"Maybe you just don't want it, and I'm the one being rude," she said softly. "I'm sure it does seem to you that I'm trying to force myself on you."

Thatch couldn't think of anything he'd like better at the moment than this woman forcing herself on him. He gazed at her. Although he'd been fooled before, he considered himself a better than average judge of character. Susan Williams was probably exactly what she seemed: an open, caring woman who was genuinely concerned about the passengers. He pried her wineglass from her hands and set it on the counter.

"I can't imagine any man being fool enough not to want your interest," he said, tilting her chin so that she had to meet his eyes. "I'm sure you know that you're very attractive and personable. I'm not used to so much attention, even if it is being done only in the line of duty. Forgive me if I've been insensitive."

The words "only in the line of duty" echoed in Susan's head, obscuring Thatch's compliment and the warmth of his fingers beneath her chin.

She resisted the urge to move his hand. If she wasn't personally interested—*foolishly* personally interested—she wouldn't subject herself to the uncertainty and insecurity he set off in her. She wasn't used to it, and she didn't like it, but she couldn't leave him alone!

"I really did come in here to have a quiet drink," she murmured, needing him to believe it.

He nodded. "I'm sure you did, and I've prevented that." He picked up his mug and finished his beer in one long gulp. Then he got off the stool. "I hope I'll see you again."

Filled with a mix of relief and regret, Susan told herself it was for the best that he was leaving. If she had any sense, she would let him go and put him out of her mind. She had a job to do, and it wasn't to chase him all over the ship.

"You probably will," she said, trying to sound indifferent. "Because I'm in charge of so many activities, I'm very visible."

Thatch was sure Susan would stand out in a crowd, whether she was in charge of activities or not. But he only nodded, then turned away.

Outside the lounge, he picked up his pace, heading back toward his room. Maybe the beer would make him sleepy. Maybe not. At least he wouldn't be in physical proximity to Susan. He halted abruptly, thinking of how downcast she'd seemed when he was sharp with her. And how pretty she'd looked when she gave him her dazzling dimpled smile.

"Hell," he muttered to himself, attracting odd gazes from other guests going down the hall. "And I do mean hell!"

Pretending to occupy herself with the wine, Susan steadied her hand enough to take another sip. It was a good thing Thatch hadn't responded as eagerly to her as she had to him. He would save her, as well as himself.

"Susan."

She froze when she heard her name. She'd almost succeeded in convincing herself that it was best Thatch had gone. She could relax at last and put things in perspective. She almost wished he hadn't come back.

Almost.

Thatch shoved his hands into his pockets when he saw the tension in Susan's shoulders. She didn't turn around at the sound of her name, although he knew she'd heard him. Why he had returned was the big question.

He knew why, of course. Aware of the inexplicable tension that had built up between him and this woman, he'd realized there in the hall that he'd never be able to sleep. He wished he hadn't stopped her initially for directions, but he had, and somehow they'd come to this awkward point.

It wasn't her fault. Hell, it wasn't his, either. He told himself there was no reason in the world that he couldn't be friendly with Susan. So what if something happened and his cover was blown?

Even private investigators took vacations. His mere presence on the ship didn't mean he was here to solve the jewelry thefts. And so what if he'd adjusted the truth in his responses to her? All of the answers were altered, yet revolved around basic facts.

Abruptly he realized that the real lies were the ones he was telling himself. He wasn't back here because he wanted to be *friendly* with this woman. It didn't take a high IQ to figure out that the tension was male-female attraction.

It didn't take brains to know that he should ignore the attraction, but he couldn't seem to do that. He had to play the hand that fate had dealt him, and that meant dealing with his attraction to Susan, no matter where it led.

"Mr. Masters made it plain that the captain won't be giving me a personal tour," he said, still talking to her back. "Would I be imposing too much to ask if you could find the time?"

Susan felt her heart speed up as she looked at Thatch. "Not at all," she said a bit breathlessly. "Just let me know when."

She was giving him another chance to save himself, but Thatch couldn't make himself take it.

"Would now be too soon? Maybe just a walk around the deck? I'm told the sea air is very soothing. It might help me sleep."

Susan's protective instincts urged her to refuse. She was too emotionally vulnerable tonight to spend any more time with Thatch. But her mind didn't register that fact fully. She heard herself agreeing with him.

"It might indeed. I'll just finish this," she said, lifting her wineglass.

"No hurry," Thatch insisted, defying his racing pulse and pounding heart. Why on God's earth was he doing this to himself?

Susan thought he might not be in a hurry, but everything inside her was at high speed. A walk would surely help her sleep, help her dispel some of this unnatural energy surging around in her because of Thatch.

He watched as she gracefully slid off the stool and came toward him. She was a mix of class and sensuality. The way she held herself suggested great pride, yet there was no stiffness in her gait. In fact, she moved her tall body with an easy motion that caused her hips to sway just enough to be enticing. He responded automatically to her beauty, no matter how he tried to slow his accelerated pulse and pounding heart.

He really was scheduled to have a tour of the ship by the captain, though no travel agent had promised it. Management had arranged it to aid him in his job.

He wondered just how much attention he could give to detail with Susan Williams as his tour guide. All he seemed able to concentrate on was her.

She was turning into one hell of a complication!

Chapter Four

Thatch wasn't really sure how he'd found himself in the elevator with Susan, en route to the Fiesta Deck. They were the only ones in the car. He reached for the number panel at the same time Susan did. Their fingers touched, his closing over hers. He withdrew his so quickly that Susan caught her breath.

"Sorry," he murmured. "Go ahead."

"No problem," Susan said, lying valiantly as she pressed the button.

There was a very big problem. If the man couldn't stand her, why was he here? She'd felt a jolt of electricity up her arm at the merest touch of his fingers on hers, but she must have been the only one. She didn't understand him at all.

Who was the real Thatch? The shy man or the sharp-tongued one? The cynic or the charmer? The one who'd left her alone in the lounge? Or the one

who'd come back for her? And why had he bothered?

Better yet, why on God's earth had she agreed to
walk with him on the deck, knowing how romantic the
sea was at night? Many a woman had lost her heart on
this very ship.

She smiled self-mockingly. She certainly wasn't going to have that problem with Thatch. The way things
were going, he wouldn't ever give her the chance to
throw her heart at him.

She wondered if that was why she persisted, bound
to involve him whether he was enthusiastic or not?
Was it because she couldn't stand being rebuffed? Or
worse, was it because she was already falling for him?

As though the ship were tired of her questions and
wanted to provide answers, it suddenly listed slightly
to the right, throwing Susan and Thatch off balance.

Thatch swiftly went into a defensive stance, legs
bent, bracing himself against the guardrail in the car
with one hand and drawing Susan tightly against his
chest with the other.

Her pounding heart echoed the beat of his. For a
single moment, she didn't dare move. She didn't want
to. She felt too good crushed against Thatch.

But, alas, she realized that he'd reacted out of fear,
and she didn't want him to be alarmed. "It's nothing
but a little rough water," she said. "We'll be fine."

Thatch looked at her, knowing she was talking,
though having one hell of a time deciphering what she
was saying. It was as if her words were coming to him
from a long distance, after the effects of her body
against his, setting him on fire, scrambling his brain.

She was much more lush than he'd imagined, her figure firm and full and stimulating. The scent of her perfume intoxicated him, the touch of her silky hair intrigued him. Her skin was like velvet against his.

"Thatch!"

His name spoken so loudly jarred him from his stupor. He blinked.

"Thatch, we're okay," Susan said with a sigh, hating more than anything to free herself from his grip, but believing that the man was almost paralyzed with fear.

She pried one of his hands from around her, and the other from the rail. Then she laughed lightly.

"You've been in California too long. Nothing's moving except the elevator, and it's going up just as it should be, working fine. I'm steady now. See?"

Planting her feet a little apart, she indicated her body, making a sweeping motion with her hands.

When Thatch followed them, he felt like groaning aloud. This woman was too tempting for a mortal man, a flawed man, a man with a penchant for blondes. He savored the sight of her, taking the opportunity to scan her from the top of her head to her feet and back up again.

Every inch looked delicious. And now Thatch knew that it *was* delicious—sinfully delicious. He didn't think he would ever forget the way she felt pressed against him, the curve of her hips, the fullness of her breasts, the...

He glanced away without a word. He was dumbfounded by Susan's ability to mesmerize him, to totally captivate his attention so that he didn't think about anything else, didn't care about anything else.

Susan shook her head. What was it about her that he didn't like? She was attractive. She was personable. She was bright. She was . . . she was apparently not his type!

She wasn't one for self-punishment. She'd had it with trying to figure Thatch out, trying to get him to take an interest in her. When the elevator halted, Susan strode out.

The man really was impossible!

She had gone part of the way down the deck when she discovered she was alone. She had been concentrating so hard that she hadn't realized Thatch wasn't beside her. She looked about. Damn him! Where had he vanished to now?

Whirling around, she stalked toward the elevator, only to bring herself up short when she saw Thatch leaning against the wall.

"What are you doing?" she asked.

"Waiting," he said evenly.

"For what?" Agitation was plain in her voice. "I thought we were going for a walk."

He nodded and idly glanced down at his nails. Susan did the same, noticing that his nails were neatly blunt cut.

"I thought so, too," he said, as if his behavior wasn't odd at all. "Yet I see that you want to walk alone. I'm waiting until you're finished. I always take a lady back to where I met her."

Crossing her arms, Susan glared at the man, wondering why on earth she was bothering with him. He was not shy. He was not tongue-tied. He was not charming. He was perverse!

"What are you talking about?" she demanded.

His bright blue eyes met her brooding brown ones. "I'm talking about your striding off and leaving me. I'll be the first one to say that you're in incredibly beautiful shape, and no doubt, being in the recreation business, you can do a mile and a half in fifteen minutes, but *I* can't."

"Is that what this is all about?" Susan shook her head again, then caught the unconscious motion and stopped. Instead, she stroked her neck in an even more betraying gesture.

"When a lady offers to take a stroll with me," Thatch murmured, "I take her at her word. If you want to race-walk, you need another partner."

"You know something, Thatch?" Susan muttered. He nodded. "A few things."

"I'm not playing," she said testily. "Do you know that you're simply too much trouble for me to bother with? If I was walking too fast, why in heaven's name didn't you say so? Why did you just stop here and hold up the wall? I didn't know what had happened to you when I didn't see you."

His gaze was as even as hers. "You were gone so fast I didn't have time to say anything."

She exhaled wearily. "Thatch, we apparently aren't going to be friends. We just don't get along and I'm not sure why. I've tried. Maybe I'm too tired to cope and maybe you really don't want to be bothered. This was a bad idea."

Defeated, Susan reached for the elevator button. They had a saying in the South about beating a dead horse. A man—and a woman—had to know when to quit. She was giving up on Thatch.

He caught her hand and drew it toward him. "It's a good idea. We're both tired. We're both uptight. We need that stroll, but let's take it *together*."

Without further ado, he tucked her hand beneath his arm and started walking at a pace much slower than hers had been. Speechless, aware of her trembling fingers against Thatch's muscular forearm, Susan did as she was told. Didn't the crazy man know that this was what she'd wanted all along?

They had been walking for about five minutes, nodding to people that they passed, moving in synchronized steps before anything was said.

"Isn't this better?" Thatch asked, although in truth he wasn't sure. It had taken him five minutes to think of something other than the fact that Susan Williams was at his side, her hand on his arm, her hip and thigh occasionally, tantalizingly, brushing his.

Susan had never felt quite like this before, never been in this position, walking beside a total stranger, her heart pounding, her pulse racing, her body burning where it touched his. Her mouth felt as if it had been stuffed with cotton. She pressed her lips together to see if they would form words. Then she attempted one.

"Yes."

Thatch glanced over at her. "Ah, such enthusiasm," he teased. "Am I wrong? Perhaps you don't think this is better. Maybe you'd rather walk at a faster pace?"

"No, this really is better," she assured him, enjoying the stroll in spite of the heady way she was feeling, or maybe because of it.

She shivered a little, and he patted her hand. "Surely you're not chilly."

"No, not at all," she said.

Quite the opposite, if the truth were told. Drawing in a steadying breath of invigorating sea air, she attempted to clear some of the cobwebs from her brain, to shove back some of the intoxicating awareness of this stranger beside her.

"I love the night air on the ocean," she said, looking out at the pitch-black water, which was visible only because the lights on the Fiesta Deck were bouncing their beams off the waves. "In fact," she added, "I love everything about the ocean."

"Do you?" he asked, intrigued by how genuine she sounded. He wanted to know more about Susan Williams. In fact, he wanted to know *all* about her. "Tell me why a lovely woman like you spends her time as a recreational director far from home—somewhere in the South, I surmise—pampering a succession of strangers."

It was the one single question sure to set Susan off, the one she and her mother argued about constantly. "I just told you," she declared too vehemently. "I love it!"

Studying her without comment, Thatch wondered why she was defensive about her job. And defensive she was. He had no doubt of that. She'd said she loved it, but with a hint of…anger—yes, that was it—in her voice. Why? The investigator in him automatically sought a motive.

Feeling uncomfortable, Susan gestured to the luxurious surroundings, the massive swimming pool, the deck chairs, the outdoor bar, the sports facilities.

"Look at all this. It's just as wonderful to me now as the first time I ever saw it," she said passionately.

She found herself thinking how odd it was that Stonehall, her family home in Charlottesville, had many of the same amenities, but she saw Stonehall as a prison rather than a refuge, just as she saw the people who frequented it as threatening, while she enjoyed the passengers on *Mexico Magic.* And on *Magic,* she didn't have her mother constantly reminding her what a disappointment she was.

Thatch frowned. "You're kidding. Everything becomes routine after a while, especially a job."

"A job?" Susan repeated, coming out of her introspection.

She didn't know why she was letting thoughts of her mother follow her onto the ship this trip, dampening her enthusiasm. Was it, she wondered, because of this man—this stranger—that she was feeling so unsettled, knowing her mother wouldn't approve of him? She had to stop thinking like that. There was no reason for her to even consider whether or not her mother would like Thatch.

"Yes, a job. That's what it is, isn't it?" Thatch asked.

"Ah," Susan mocked, trying to lighten the dark mood overtaking her, "now who's lacking in enthusiasm? You sound jaded, Thatch. Perhaps your job isn't fulfilling, but mine is. Besides, it's more like an adventure, a fantasy time."

She squeezed his arm. "I was serious when I said I was willing to bet you'd say you'd had the time of your life when this trip is over. If you don't tell me it was, then my name's not Susan Williams."

Thatch had to smile. There was no hint of anger now. Her voice practically purred with her love of the ship, her drawl stretching every word.

"Are you from the South, Susan?" he asked.

"You know I am by my accent," she said. "It's really evident when I'm annoyed or distressed."

"Or excited?"

She smiled slightly. "I suppose."

"I'll remember that," he said, winking at her.

"You won't have to remember it. You'll hear the syrupy thickness. I can't seem to avoid it. At least not yet, but I'm working on it."

"That would be a shame," Thatch murmured. "Your voice is very appealing, a little husky, making it sexy, a little lilting, making it pleasant to the ears, and different with that drawl and carefully enunciated words."

Well, Susan thought, it seemed he'd found something he liked about her. A voice wasn't much, but it was a start!

"Thank you," she said, very conscious of her voice now. "Thank you very much."

"You're welcome. Very welcome."

He couldn't stop staring at her. She was an enigma to him. He wondered if she'd ever traveled on a ship before she took the job. She sounded cultured and moneyed, but maybe it was an acquired class, not one born and bred. He decided not to pursue the topic, even though he wanted to know. Her response to why she worked on the ship warned him away from getting too personal too soon.

"Do you live in Los Angeles?" Susan asked, knowing that just because he'd boarded there didn't mean he lived there.

He nodded. "I'm one of those rare people—a native Californian." He chuckled. "On second thought, maybe they aren't so rare anymore, though most are still imports. Everything in California is in a perpetual state of flux, always changing."

Susan smiled. "That's more than I can say for the South. Sometimes it seems to me that nothing changes. My mother..."

Her words trailed off as she unconsciously crossed her arms. Her mother again! She wasn't about to tell Thatch that her mother was still trying to right a wrong that happened forty years ago! That Julia was trying to reconstruct her life through her daughter, that she was trying to force her daughter into the South's own peculiar caste system, where both name and money—*old* money and *old* family name—were what counted!

Julia had succeeded in giving Susan both: now she wanted her daughter to splash herself on every society page, to make the match of the century, to impress all the people who'd shunned Julia when she was still Julia Harriston, before her marriage to Jonathan Williams.

"Yes?" Thatch prodded, curious to know more. He hadn't missed her withdrawal.

She shrugged. "My mother doesn't like change." That hadn't been what she was going to say and they both knew it. She would have been more truthful saying her mother lived in the past.

"Does she like ship travel?" Thatch asked. "Has she ever been on a ship where you were working?"

Susan's laughter was without merriment. Her mother wouldn't be caught dead on a ship where her daughter was doing "menial" labor.

"No, she hasn't."

Sensing the shift in her mood, Thatch didn't press her about her mother, either. He didn't want anything more to spoil this evening. He wanted this one time with Susan to be special, for he knew he couldn't—no, *mustn't*—spend time with her again, alone like this. He was too interested. Much too interested.

"What about your family?" Susan asked, hoping to deflect the subject from her to him. "Did you follow in your father's footsteps in the insurance business?"

Thatch hesitated. This was just one of the reasons he shouldn't be here with her. He hated lying to her, even if they were white lies.

"No. My father was a mechanic and my mother was—still is—an assembly-line worker in a manufacturing company."

"Oh," Susan said, surprised without quite knowing why. She'd suspected Thatch might come from a wealthy background. The fact that he'd won a trip usually indicated someone who was a big business achiever, even though he'd said he'd won because he hadn't missed any work. Workaholics were usually very successful. Besides, he just seemed so worldly, so cosmopolitan, despite his contradictory Jekyll-and-Hyde personality.

"Oh, what?" he said, hearing the surprise in her voice. Surely she wasn't attracted to him because she thought he was wealthy! On the other hand, it wasn't impossible, considering the situation. He knew that those least in need of free trips in a company were the ones who generally won them—the driven, ambitious people.

While he did just fine in his business, he wasn't wealthy, and he didn't come from a moneyed background. He liked that to be made clear right from the start with a woman. That was another lesson left over from the affair gone bad with the blond client.

Susan glanced at him and shrugged. "Oh, nothing," she said, avoiding his eyes, suddenly reminded that this stroll might just be a tiny romantic idyll never to be repeated. The thought made her a little sad.

"Is your family wealthy?" Thatch asked, seeing how Susan seemed to dismiss him, her eyes going to the water again.

"Why would you think that?" she asked.

He shrugged. "I didn't say I did. I'm just asking. In case you don't know it, you're one classy woman. Good breeding has a certain air, which perhaps can be acquired, yet I suspect in your case is inbred. You've got that kind of class."

"Thank you," she said, her voice cool. She wasn't mistaken. Something about the way Thatch had asked about her family reminded her of Charles, and Charles's obsession with money bothered her.

"You know," she said bitterly, "too many people are too concerned with money and what it can bring, both materially and socially."

"Are you directing that observation at me personally?" Thatch asked, unaware of how bitter he himself sounded earlier. Susan glanced away, unwilling to square off against him on the subject of wealth. "Actually," she murmured evasively, partly in truth, "I was thinking of Charles Masters."

A frown creased Thatch's brow. Charles Masters. That was yet another reason he shouldn't be here with this woman. He couldn't forget the sight of Susan in Charles's arms. In fact, he realized only this moment, he'd been a little jealous.

"Are you and Charles—as they say so quaintly in L.A.—an item?" he inquired.

"No," Susan answered quickly. "We're friends." She didn't know why she sounded so defensive. That was the extent of her relationship with Charles as far as she was concerned.

Although Thatch noticed the hesitation, he wasn't sure what to make of it.

Feeling suddenly drained by the reminder not only of her mother, but of Charles, too, Susan decided she'd spent enough time with this exciting stranger for one night. There would be other opportunities when they were both more rested.

At least she hoped there would be.

"I do believe you're right about the walk," Thatch said, his mind turning to the job he'd been hired to do at the mention of Charles. Masters wasn't the only one who wanted to be rich. There was probably a thief aboard ship who had aspirations along that line—illegal aspirations.

"How am I right?" Susan asked, interrupting Thatch's reverie.

"I think I can sleep now," he explained. "Are you ready to turn in?"

"Great minds..." Susan murmured. "I was about to suggest the same thing."

He smiled. "Good. We're in accord on something."

Susan wanted to proclaim that they weren't so terribly mismatched, but she didn't. In truth, it was too early to tell how suited they were. Much too early.

"I'll see you to your room," Thatch said.

"Oh, that's not necessary," Susan replied, heading toward the first elevator.

He chuckled. "Then maybe you'd better see me to mine. We're at the opposite end of the ship from where we started, aren't we?"

Susan laughed. "Oh, good heavens, we are. You're right. I'll see you to your room. I don't want you roaming the halls all night looking for it."

Thatch grinned. "Thank you. I like a woman who takes good care of a man."

Susan was feeling overly warm again, and she didn't think it was from the walk. She truly did need rest. It had been a long day.

When the elevator stopped on Thatch's floor, she pointed down the hall. "That way," she said. "Take three right turns, and that should put you close enough to your door that you can find it."

"Hey, no fair," he protested. "You said you'd see me to my door."

"I lied," she said. "I'm too tired to walk all the way down there, then back to my room."

"Well, that's a fine how-do-you-do!" he teased. "Some escort you turn out to be. Where is your room, anyway?"

"Down in the bowels of the ship with the rest of the plebeian help," she said, smiling. "I'm on the Glorioso Deck—Spanish for glorious. Do you speak Spanish?" she asked, the thought not having occurred to her before, even though she knew that many people who took the Mexico cruise did.

"A word or two," Thatch said, once more finding himself in the position—a well-known one—of lying and, for whatever reason, hating to lie to Susan Williams. He simply couldn't afford to be open with her.

Actually he spoke Spanish quite well, since it was a common language in California and he'd lived in the state all his life.

Susan smiled. "Well, if I can be of any help, let me know, but I warn you, I took a crash course on Spanish-English tapes, and I speak only the barest minimum."

He looked puzzled. "It really isn't necessary to know Spanish for this cruise, is it?"

"No, of course not," she said, "but the Mexicans love to bargain. When we go ashore, I may be of help to you since I know enough of the language and customs to save you some money if you shop."

He shook his head. "Not to worry. I'm not the shopping type." He indicated his clothes. "I didn't want to go out and buy even these. However, I felt I should dress appropriately for the cruise, whatever that means."

Thatch nearly bit his tongue. Lies and more lies! Why didn't he just shut up? Why was he trying to tell the woman that he didn't normally wear flowered shirts and deck shoes, for crying out loud?

It was a rhetorical question. He knew why. He knew that some day he was going to have to tell her that he was a fraud. That he was in disguise, from his flowered shirts to his name.

And it bothered him.

Damn it to hell! He'd already broken his cardinal rule. He was becoming personally involved with this woman.

And that made him a fool of the first order. Maybe even worse. It could jeopardize this case.

For a few minutes he pondered abandoning the job and letting his partner, who was on board, take over completely. But he knew he wouldn't do that. He wasn't a quitter. He didn't give up until he got his man.

Or woman.

His brow creased in a frown as he pondered the situation.

Susan laughed. "Don't worry. You look great."

And that was the truth, she told herself. The blue flowered shirt did nothing at all to disguise his blatant masculinity. If anything, it contrasted and accented it. His slacks and deck shoes only made his lean hips, long legs and virility more obvious.

Susan had to think about something else! "We don't have any clothing requirements—at least for the passengers. People generally dress for the Captain's Dinner, for the Christmas Eve party and the New Year's Eve party. Other than that, anything goes. The suits you wear on the job are fine if you're more comfortable in them."

Thatch forced a grin. He owned exactly three suits, and he had two of them with him.

"I don't think my room would accommodate them," he said wryly.

Susan smiled. "The rooms are small, but *Mexico Magic* itself is relatively small. That's what allows us the opportunity to give our passengers the personal touch. And anyway, the ship is beautifully done, don't you think?"

"What I've seen of it," he agreed.

"Tell you what," she said. "Come to the water-exercise class in the morning, and afterward I'll give you more of a tour. I want you to see the gym where aerobics is taught. I also teach ballroom dancing. I'll show you the studio."

Thatch hedged. This had to stop. He couldn't let this woman continue to entice him. He was all too willing.

Seeing his reluctance, Susan clasped his hands. "Do come, Thatch. You'll enjoy the session, I promise. The exercise class is held on the deck we just left—the Fiesta. The pool is huge, the water is warm, the participants amiable. It'll be fun."

A vision of how this sexy beauty must look in a bathing suit filled his mind. Thatch didn't know if he could stand it. Or if he should even try.

"I don't know," he said, remembering that she'd said she was a toucher and trying not to draw away. His hands were damp. He couldn't believe it. She had him, literally, right in the palm of her hand!

"I'm not much on water exercises," he muttered.

"Come on," she coaxed, her pretty mouth pouting. "Don't let me down. I want to involve you." She squeezed his fingers. "Pretty please. Say you'll come."

Thatch's gaze was inexorably drawn to that full mouth of hers. He wanted to involve her, too. Before he thought about what he was doing, he pressed the button to close the elevator doors, slipped his arms around Susan's waist, bent down and kissed her.

Responding as if it was the most natural thing in the world, Susan wrapped her arms around his neck and returned the provocative caress of his warm lips.

Thatch groaned at the exquisite pleasure of her mouth on his. She felt even more wonderful than he'd expected. He couldn't recall ever holding a more enchanting woman in his arms, or responding to a kiss so passionately. He couldn't seem to draw her close enough.

Susan felt her breasts tighten against Thatch's chest. His arms held her fiercely, crushing her against the hard lines of his body, causing a strange kind of good ache within her. She was breathless from this demanding kiss, yet she wanted more.

When his tongue sought the tender inside of her mouth, she welcomed it, parting her lips so that he might penetrate more easily. The gesture seemed to drive Thatch to deeper depths of desire.

His hands sought Susan's soft curves, stealing down her hips as she hungrily sampled his mouth and tongue. When he cupped her derriere, pulling her fiercely against him, Susan was stirred from her passion.

They were moving much too fast here. And much too boldly. She didn't know what had gotten into her.

She shouldn't be indulging in this steamy behavior, no matter how much Thatch intoxicated her. She hardly knew the man. She didn't want him to get the wrong idea.

And any moment, another passenger might press the button for the car. It was evident to anyone with a grain of sense that she had been thoroughly kissed and caressed.

"Thatch . . ." she whispered against his lips.

"Mmm," he murmured. "Sweet, sweet Susan. I never expected this much special attention in my wildest dreams."

He did have the wrong idea, she realized, and it was no wonder! Well, not exactly the wrong idea, she corrected herself, thinking that she'd enjoyed this as much as he had, but this was too much of a good thing too soon for her to be comfortable.

"Thatch," she tried again, pushing against his shoulders. "We need to call it a night."

He stared down at her from passion-glazed eyes.

She looked embarrassed. "We—I—don't want to give you the wrong idea."

"Wrong idea?" he repeated inanely.

She nodded. "I don't usually—I mean . . ."

Oh, good grief! What *did* she mean? She'd all but invited him into her arms, and when he took her up on the invitation, she'd withdrawn it. She *didn't* want him to get the wrong idea, but she didn't know how to explain it in the right way, now that she'd chased him.

And that was what she'd done!

Thatch gazed at her a moment longer, then released her. The woman was giving him another chance to flee from her many charms, and it was a chance he should take—posthaste! If she hadn't stopped him, he would have done his best to make love to her right there in the elevator. And to hell with his job!

"Right," he said tersely, knowing he should say more, but unable to come up with anything.

When Susan looked bewildered, he wanted to draw her back into his arms and hold her. And that would be incredibly stupid!

"Sorry," he said. "I didn't mean to get out of line."

Then he stepped from the elevator and strode rapidly away. Susan was left to stare after him in dismay. He did have the wrong idea, and she didn't know what to do about it.

She gasped when a couple entered the car.

"Is something wrong?" the woman asked.

Susan shook her head. "No," she murmured. "I was just daydreaming. I didn't expect anyone."

The woman looked down the hall as the man pushed a deck number and the doors began to close.

Susan's gaze followed the other woman's in time to see Thatch turn the corner.

What had she done? she asked herself. Dear Lord, what had she done?

Chapter Five

Susan was so wrapped up in her thoughts that she didn't see Charles standing outside her room until she almost crashed into him.

"Charles," she gasped, "what are you doing here?"

"Waiting for you," he said dryly. "Where have you been? I checked everywhere."

Not everywhere, she thought. Still, she didn't want to encourage one of Charles's tantrums. "I was walking on the Fiesta Deck, hoping to unwind enough to sleep."

"I thought you had a headache and wanted to go to bed an hour ago," he said, his voice accusing.

Susan glanced at her watch. She was amazed to discover that she'd been with Thatch an hour! "I didn't realize it was so late," she answered truthfully. "I knew I couldn't sleep until I did something physical."

Her fingers automatically went to her lips as she thought about the particular physical thing she'd done with Thatch. Her mouth was still tingling.

Glaring at her suspiciously, Charles remarked, "Surely you weren't with that—what's his name?— Thatcher."

Although Susan was caught unprepared by the question, she decided not to deny that she'd been with Thatch. She knew she would see him again if she got the chance—though that was doubtful now.

"In fact, I was. He needed to relax, and so did I. As I said, something physical helps me sleep, so we went for a walk."

Even though he'd asked, Charles clearly didn't expect her answer. "You didn't actually go strolling about the decks with that man, did you?"

"Yes," she said, lifting her chin a degree. "I did. So what?"

"So what?" he asked tightly. "You don't know a thing about him. He seems rather shady to me. I don't like your spending time with him alone."

"You're my boss, not my keeper," Susan retorted. "Please don't presume to tell me whom to see."

"Someone has to! As your boss, I'll tell you that you have a certain image to keep up as a ship employee, and a woman who dashes about the decks with odd men at all hours of the night isn't the right one. Maybe management had a point, after all. Perhaps you are too young for this job. I can't believe you took up with that man the first night at sea."

"I did not 'take up with him'!" Susan shot back hotly, knowing she was overreacting because of what had happened between her and Thatch. She just wanted to go to bed and forget tonight—at least some parts of it. "And don't you dare say that maybe management was wrong to give me the job!" she continued, her brown eyes brooding. "I'm very good at what I do, and you know it."

"Maybe," Charles said, relenting slightly, "but you don't know anything about people. If that man's not a fortune hunter, I'm not Charles Masters."

"A fortune hunter? Thatch?" Susan asked incredulously. "I hate to disillusion you, Charles, but he seems to resent the rich as much as you do!"

A stunned look crossed Charles's face. "Don't tell me you told the man you're rich!"

"Of course not!" she snapped. Suddenly Susan couldn't stand to hear any more. "Go to bed, Charles," she said, reaching for the key to her room. "That's what I'm going to do. I'm very, very tired."

Charles pulled her back around and grasped her shoulders, his fingers biting into them. "Fine. See that you go to bed and not back up to the Fiesta Deck. I'm really shocked by your behavior—and your deceit," he said in a low, hard voice.

"I did nothing deceitful," she said, prying his fingers from her shoulders. "Take your hands off me, Charles!"

His face a mask of anger, he obviously had more to say, but he swallowed hard and let her go. "Don't be foolish, Susan," he said. "I'll show you what kind of man Thatcher is. I've seen his type on board plenty of times, and so have you. All I need to do is have a little chat with him about his integrity, or lack of it."

"You're joking!" she exclaimed. "What gives you the right to even bring up such a topic with Thatch?"

Charles shrugged. "I'll come up with something—like maybe I suspect him of being the burglar."

Susan's mouth fell open. "Don't be absurd," she said, her voice rising. "He hasn't been on any of the ships that were burglarized."

Charles made a careless gesture with his hands. "How do I know he didn't have an accomplice on them, doing the dirty work for him? I wouldn't be at all surprised if he lives right there in L.A., making it oh-so-convenient to be involved. Now that Laurent is gone, the main man might have to come forward. And that's what we all want, isn't it?"

Susan shook her head. "I don't believe this. As far as we know, the thefts have stopped with Laurent. You're behaving horribly, and without justification. Talk about driving away passengers! A talk with Thatch about his integrity or your suspicions could do worse than that, for heaven's sake. I don't know what's gotten into you."

"What's gotten into *me?*" he returned. "What about *you?* Why, all of a sudden, are you taking an unprecedented—and reckless—interest in a total stranger who's one of hundreds who've traveled on *Magic?*"

"Why, you're jealous! That's what's wrong with you," Susan cried. "Oh, Charles, don't do this. I've told you I am not romantically interested in you. I have the right to see any man I choose."

"I'm not jealous!" he insisted. "I'm trying to watch out for you."

"Don't!" she flung at him, moving away. "As I said, go to bed."

Then she inserted the key and went into her room. She had almost succeeded in shutting the door when Charles blocked it with his foot.

"As *I* said, Susan, don't be foolish."

Susan felt her temper rising and knew she had to get control of this situation. She had no intention of battling with the man all night. She opened the door a little wider, as if she were going to let him enter.

When he moved his foot, she quickly slammed the door. "Good night, Charles," she said. "Get some rest. You really need it, too."

Even though the halls were carpeted, she could hear Charles's angry movements as he left. Breathing a sigh of relief, she walked over to her bed and sat down. This had been one of the longest days of her life. And one of the most tumultuous.

Charles had upset her more than she wanted to admit, for he'd verbalized some of the fears that had been cropping up in her own mind. Her attraction to Thatch *was* unprecedented and reckless!

She had enough to worry about with Charles and her mother, and the possibility that the thefts hadn't stopped on *Magic*. Thatch was another complication in her life she didn't need.

A complication—and the most exciting thing that had ever happened to her!

In his room, Thatch paced restlessly. He didn't know what on God's earth had prompted him to kiss Susan. That was another lie, he quickly confessed—he knew *exactly* what had prompted it. Still, he hadn't meant to do it. He exhaled heavily. Now that he'd done it, all he could think of was doing it again.

He shuddered as he reminded himself that he'd behaved carelessly and unprofessionally. He'd let his own desire get in the way. And now what? Did he avoid her? Or did he keep a discreet distance and pretend the kiss had never happened?

"Hell," he muttered aloud. He was really messing up this job. He had to get on course. He looked down at his watch. He was scheduled to meet Eva, his partner, in the dining room for the midnight buffet.

Going to his luggage, he withdrew the staff files and sat down to go over them. Perhaps if he could concentrate on something besides Susan, he could begin to form a concrete plan for catching the thief—whoever he or she was.

When Thatch looked at his watch again, he was irked to realize he'd stayed in his room too long. He'd been so caught up in the information—Susan's history, in particular—that he'd lost track of time.

It appeared that Susan Williams *was* rich. He didn't know why the thought stunned him. He'd run into all kinds of people with all sorts of reasons for doing things, and a wealthy young woman working on a cruise ship wasn't the most unusual by any stretch of the imagination. He had told her himself that she was a woman of class.

No wonder, since she was the daughter of Jonathan Stonehall Williams, so wealthy and so well-known that even Thatch had heard of him. There were articles in the financial papers when Jonathan Stonehall Williams died. He'd been much older than his wife Julia, and had left one daughter, Susan Williams.

She and the assistant recreational director on *Mexico Magic* were one and the same. The woman who'd inherited, if Thatch recalled correctly, controlling interest in J.S.W. Textiles.

Immediately, Thatch's mind shifted into high gear as he dealt with a string of *what if*s. What if the company was in financial trouble? What if Jonathan Stonehall Williams had mishandled the company and only his death had exposed the mismanagement? What if Julia Williams had squandered the assets after Jonathan's death? What if Susan—

He instantly dismissed the forming question. Susan was not involved in the jewelry thefts. He would stake his life on it.

But was that only because he wanted to believe it?

No, something inside him, some intangible knowledge, assured him that the woman wasn't culpable. Anyway, the jewelry stolen was valuable, but not valuable enough to make a huge company solvent, if that was the problem. Still, what if there was some connection?

He shook his head, instinctively knowing that the Williams fortune didn't have anything to do with the thefts, but there was still the matter of Susan not admitting who she was. However, there were many possible explanations for that, the least of which was that such wealth made her vulnerable in a special way.

Thatch glanced at his watch again. He didn't have time to mull over the implications of Susan's wealth or work. He'd already spent too much time on her file as it was, combing through her documented life as if his own depended on it.

And it might—if Susan was involved in the burglaries. He closed his mind to the suggestion. He wouldn't even indulge that possibility—it was too absurd.

His smile was bitter. *That* was how dangerous and incautious his reasoning was. He did not believe the woman was involved in any fashion, shape or form. He seriously doubted that anything less than a slap in the face with evidence he saw with his own eyes would convince him otherwise.

After quickly shoving the files back into the secret compartment of his luggage, he strode from the room. Eva would be wondering where he was.

By the time he reached the dining room, it was filled with people enjoying a seemingly endless and delectable-looking assortment of food, from Mexican fare to American, laid out on several tables. From a far corner of the room, Thatch scanned the crowd but didn't see Eva.

He stiffened when he caught sight of Merry Lou Addison. Damn his bad luck for meeting up with her! He watched her for a few minutes, then exhaled wearily—he hadn't realized how tense he was till then. Merry Lou had, thank God, found a companion. She was laughing with an older gentleman, taking amusingly dainty bites from his plate, or accepting them from his fingers.

"I'll meet you up on the Fiesta Deck."

Thatch tensed when the woman spoke to him. He had to pull himself together, he thought or he wasn't going to be worth a damn on this job. If he hadn't recognized Eva's voice, he wouldn't have known that the woman who'd spoken was her. They'd agreed not

to call each other's rooms, just to be on the safe side
against the eager ears of cabin boys.

Dressed in a lovely blue dress and matching high
heels, her gray hair done up in a halo of curls for the
occasion, Eva walked on. Thatch stared after her in
amazement. The woman was sixty-two years old, and
though he'd seen her in many guises, he'd never seen
her glamorous. She'd been transformed for the cruise.

He killed a few more minutes, wandering by the
buffet tables, wishing he had time to sample the food.
His stomach was growling. He didn't remember when
he'd last eaten.

He wrapped a pastry in a napkin, shoved it into his
pocket, then left. In the elevator, he began to remove
the treat, but several people joined him. They were
talking about the buffet, making Thatch hungrier and
even more aware of the dessert in his pocket.

When he arrived on the Fiesta Deck, also the destination of one of the couples, he let them depart first.
Then he pulled the sweet from his pocket, unwrapped
it and strolled toward some deck chairs, relishing each
bite of the flaky pastry.

Eva was standing alone at the railing beyond the
pool, a light breeze blowing the full skirt of her dress.
Thatch passed her.

"My word, what a beauty," he murmured softly,
only half teasing the ageless woman.

Eva chuckled as she casually looked over her
shoulder, then turned back to the sea. "I've been
hunting for you for half an hour," she said, speaking
as softly as he had. "Compliments won't assuage my
anger," she said with pretended hauteur.

Now it was Thatch's turn to chuckle as he settled down on a lounge chair, stretching out as he ate the last morsel of the pastry.

"I was engrossed in the employee files."

They fell silent at the sounds of laughter and footsteps. Eva turned from the rail, brushed at her hair and smiled at the couple who strolled by arm in arm.

"Lovely night, isn't it?" she said to them.

The pretty young woman looked at her male companion. "Lovely," she agreed, her eyes glowing. He grinned, and they walked on.

Eva waited a moment before she spoke. "Did you bring the necklace I'm supposed to wear to the Captain's Dinner?" she murmured, her gaze on the happy couple.

As Thatch watched the man and woman, he found himself thinking that a short time before he'd been walking on this very deck with Susan. He forced his attention back to Eva before he became lost in the memory.

"Would I ever be so negligent as to leave a crucial item behind?" he asked.

Eva smiled. "No. Not you. They don't call you Thorough Thatch for nothing, do they?"

Thatch slid off the lounge chair and walked toward her. "And they don't call you the Gray Ghost for nothing, do they?"

"No," she said, looking back at the black ocean. "I saw you with that blonde earlier."

"Where?" Thatch couldn't believe that Eva had seen him and he hadn't seen her! Worse, he didn't want to think that Eva had seen him strolling with

Susan. As ridiculous as it sounded, even to him, he felt his privacy had been violated.

He had to smile wryly at his double standard. He knew all about spying on people, but he didn't like being on the other side.

Eva brushed back her curls as the breeze tugged playfully at them. "On this deck. It seems to be a popular place for lovers."

"Why, you sly devil, you don't miss a trick, do you?" Thatch asked. "Not even me with a gorgeous woman who's bound to be trouble even if she isn't thief trouble."

Eva frowned. "What on earth are you talking about?"

Thatch lowered his head as he balled up the napkin that had held the dessert. "Nothing really. I'm talking like the private eyes in the movies. I believe I'm being taken in by a blond bombshell I just met, my brain's turning to mush, my heart melting into a puddle right before the woman's brown eyes."

Clearly relieved, Eva chortled. "Thatch, I don't think you have a heart, so don't try to tell me some woman—any woman—has gotten to you, especially one who could be a suspect and whom you've only just met. This is Eva you're talking to."

Thatch walked over to the railing and looked down at the water, not particularly enjoying the slight rocking motion of the ship.

"Yes," he murmured. "Eva Adkins, the best female private eye in the game, but a *woman* all the same," he teased.

"Oh-ho!" Eva returned. "Don't you try that chauvinistic stuff on me! I've been around too long to put up with it. I'll match my wits with yours in this business any day, and probably come out the winner.''

Thatch's spontaneous laughter escaped before he could smother it. "I don't doubt it, and I have no intention of humiliating myself trying to find out. You're one of the best, no question about it. You can play every part from fumbling bag lady to elegant grandam. But *I* can still get your goat!''

"You smarty-pants young whippersnapper," she joked, "you'd better watch your tongue. I'll solve this case while you're still flitting about the deck with pretty women.''

"Woman," he corrected, an image of Susan surging relentlessly into his mind. "Eva," he continued softly, "what if the unthinkable happened and I did become involved with a woman—''

Eva put her hands together in a prayerful pose before he could finish. "I'd get down on my knees and thank God you're finally ready to explore the good side of life instead of the ugly side,'' she teased.

"You didn't let me finish," he said. "If I did become involved with a woman and she turned out to be the guilty party in a case. Do you know how dangerous that could be for us all, not to mention ruining the investigation?''

Eva spoke low and solemnly. "Thatch, are you kidding? You haven't gone and done something totally stupid, have you?''

The alarm in her voice made him more aware of the ramifications of such an act. He managed a small smile. "Which question do you want me to answer first?''

Eva didn't smile. "They're equally serious, aren't they?"

"Yes," he agreed, "and no, of course I haven't done anything stupid." He hadn't, he assured himself. Reckless, maybe, but not stupid. *Yet.*

"I'm just speculating," he added.

Eva wasn't fooled. Thatch should have known she was too smart for that.

"Don't lose your grip amid the glamour of your surroundings," she murmured. "That's for tourists who pay their money, not people to whom money is paid to do a job. There's a time and place for everything, and now isn't your time for love."

"Eva," he whispered, "surely you don't think I'm that big a fool, do you?"

Eva moved closer. "Stranger things have happened. You're an excellent private eye, Thatch, but first of all you're a man. Don't go and do anything crazy, okay?"

Thatch covertly pulled a pearl necklace from his pants pocket and let it trail off his fingertips, down the leg of his pants to the deck.

Immediately he bent down to retrieve it. "I think you dropped this, madam," he said, effectively ending the personal conversation.

Eva held out her hand. "Why, thank you. I didn't even notice it was gone."

"Here, allow me," Thatch said.

Eva turned so that he could clamp the necklace at the back of her neck.

Thatch hoped she didn't feel his hands shaking. His partner had verbalized his own worst fears. He didn't have only himself to worry about. They were both at risk if he lost his head over a beautiful blonde. A beautiful blonde with brown eyes, a gorgeous figure and a winning smile.

Stifle it, Thatch! he ordered sternly. He was letting his imagination run away with him.

Susan had started around the corner when she saw the man and woman. She recognized Thatch in an instant, but then she was sure she would recognize him anywhere. She stopped in her tracks, frowning.

What was he doing out here this late? He'd said he was turning in. Despite the popularity of the Fiesta Deck, most people on their first night at sea were too weary to enjoy it. If they managed to stay up for the buffet, they were usually sated and ready for sleep.

She desperately wished she'd been. She'd eaten a sandwich in her room and drank a glass of milk after she left Thatch and finally got Charles away from her door. But it hadn't done any good. Her mind was full of Thatch and the kiss.

Because she'd experienced the futility of tossing and turning too many times, she'd decided to walk on the deck again, hoping to wear herself out. She had classes to teach tomorrow. If she had any hope of being energetic, she had to get some sleep.

Watching as Thatch stood behind the older woman, Susan tried to see if he was putting the woman's necklace on, taking it off, or what. She was caught in a moment of indecision that caused her heart to pound erratically.

She'd been sure that Thatch wouldn't know anyone on board. But of course that notion was silly. She'd seen friends and relatives run into each other, not

knowing they were taking the same cruise. Maybe
Thatch had found, like Susan, that he couldn't sleep,
after all.

But even if he couldn't, wasn't it too much of a coincidence that he was here with an older woman—
from all appearances a *wealthy* older woman—and
why was he doing whatever he was doing to her jewelry?

Charles's words echoed in her head. Was Thatch a
shady character? Was he...

She wouldn't even allow herself to indulge in the ridiculous thought that Thatch could possibly be the
thief. Damn Charles for unsettling her so! Easing back
around the corner, she started toward the elevator.

She didn't want to see any more. She didn't want to
think any more. She wished she'd never come up here.
Her fingers trembling, Susan pressed the button for
the car.

Thatch had told himself that he wasn't going to attend the exercise class Susan was teaching, but he
found himself waking up with precisely that thought
in mind. They had left each other under such strained
circumstances last night. He had lain in bed for hours
thinking about the kiss that had almost been his un-
doing, the woman who had almost caused his unrav-
eling.

Searching in his luggage, which he still hadn't put
away—a habit from moving about quickly and seeing
no need to unpack, despite Susan's saying that was one
of the big advantages of ship travel—he found his navy
blue swimsuit. When he had taken a shower and
groomed himself, he put on the trunks, wrapped a

towel around his shoulders and headed for the Fiesta Deck.

He knew at once that he'd made another mistake when he saw Susan doing warm-ups. Other passengers had beaten Thatch there, and they were gathered around the edges of the pool to watch the blond woman, in a functional one-piece black suit that did absolutely nothing to conceal her stunning figure. In fact, Thatch told himself, it accented every shapely curve, from bosom to thigh.

"Good morning."

He turned when Eva appeared, looking attractive in her own one-piece suit. "Good morning," he said simply.

Eva sat down beside him, dangling her feet in the water as she spoke loudly enough for everyone to hear. "You do remember me, don't you? The clasp came loose on my necklace last night on this very deck and I nearly lost my heirloom pearls. You found them."

Pretending to recall, Thatch gazed at Eva. "Yes, of course," he said. "Glad to be of help."

"*I* was glad you were of help," Eva said, her voice rising. "That necklace belonged to my grandmother. I would have been devastated if I had lost it. The pearls were individually selected in Japan by my grandfather."

More lies, Thatch found himself thinking in an uncharacteristic pang of guilty conscience, one that was surging to the surface more frequently since he'd come aboard. He'd purchased the necklace from a shop in L.A. just before getting on the ship.

He glanced at Susan at the other end of the pool. She was doing leg scissors and seemed totally engrossed in the movements, but he suspected she'd heard the conversation. He suspected everyone had.

That was the point, wasn't it?

Susan met Thatch's eyes as she ended the warm-up. She was filled with relief at having overheard the comments between him and the older woman she'd seen him with last night. Of course there was a logical explanation. She'd known there would be.

She included all the people gathering around the pool in her greeting. "Good morning!" she said, her smile bright, her voice lively. "I'm happy to see so many of you here on the first day. It's a great day for waking up those lazy muscles and getting ready for the splendid outings we have planned for you. When we go ashore at Puerto Vallarta, you'll want those legs in good working order."

"Doesn't that sound exciting?" Eva asked, her question directed at Thatch.

Lost in his thoughts of Miss Susy Sunshine, Thatch only nodded. Susan was the only thing he found exciting, the only thing he could think of.

When an older man standing behind them spoke, Thatch managed to nudge himself out of his Susan-induced stupor.

"*I'm* looking forward to it." The vigorous, cultured voice sang with the remnants of a British accent.

Eva and Thatch both turned to look at the man. A dapper older gentleman wearing sandals, slacks and a white shirt, he had a head of silver hair and a rakish handlebar mustache.

He beamed as he held out his hand to Eva. "I'm Sir Roger Nester, and who, may I have the pleasure of knowing, are you, lovely young lady?"

Eva glowed so brightly that Thatch wondered if it was an act or a genuine reaction to the handsome man's flattery. "I'm Eva Adkins, from Los Angeles, and I'm hardly a *young* lady, but thank you."

Sir Roger's green eyes sparkled. "You can't be a day over fifty, and you are lovely." He let his gaze skim admiringly over Eva's well-preserved body in the blue bathing suit.

She pretended to be flustered so well that Thatch began to wonder if he would need to have the same talk with her as she'd had with him about her purpose for being on the ship.

Before she could reply to the man's continued flattery, Susan called out, "Everybody in the pool!"

"Why aren't you suited up for exercise?" Eva asked Sir Roger.

He winked at her. "Old war wounds, my dear. I don't bare this body, but I do get around."

"Oh," was all Eva said. She gave Sir Roger a coy smile before slipping into the water.

Resisting the urge to shake his head, Thatch joined her in the pool but moved some distance away. From the corner of his eye, he watched Sir Roger squat down behind Eva so that he could still talk to her.

Charles appeared out of nowhere and Thatch saw Susan nod to him. In moments, music with a jazzy beat filled the morning air.

"All right, now!" Susan called out, her voice full of encouragement and animation as she motioned to the group. "Let's begin."

Thatch could hardly do the workout because he was so preoccupied with Susan and the others. His determination to keep his mind on business flagged constantly at the sight of the blond instructor, but he mustered enough wherewithal to assess those passengers participating in the water exercises, and those on the sidelines, such as Sir Roger Nester.

Half an hour later, his limbs tingling from the workout, Thatch climbed out of the water when Susan announced the end of the session. Pretending to be oblivious to Sir Roger helping Eva out of the water, Thatch reached for a towel and briskly dried himself. Susan had wrapped a towel around her body, sarong-style, by the time Thatch reached her.

"Good morning, Susan. I must say that was some workout!"

Susan smiled at him as if she were noticing him for the first time, although she'd hardly been able to keep her eyes off him during the exercises. He was even better-looking in the brief swimsuit than he'd been fully clothed. He was one of those men who was clearly comfortable with his body, with his masculinity, from his muscular hairy chest to his high-arched feet. Susan wondered how she'd ever thought of him as a bashful boy.

"Good morning. I'm glad you decided to come," she said cordially, grateful he'd made the first move. She really hadn't known what to expect.

"I only did it to see you," he said with more honesty than he'd intended. "Will you have breakfast with me?"

He hadn't known he would ask that. He'd only known he had to talk with her.

NO RISK, NO OBLIGATION TO BUY... NOW OR EVER!

GUARANTEED

PLAY "ROLL A DOUBLE" AND GET AS MANY AS SIX GIFTS!

HERE'S HOW TO PLAY:

1. Peel off label from front cover. Place it in space provided at right. With a coin, carefully scratch off the silver dice. This makes you eligible to receive one or more free books, and possibly other gifts, depending on what is revealed beneath the scratch-off area.

2. You'll receive brand-new Silhouette Romance™ novels. When you return this card, we'll rush you the books and gifts you qualify for ABSOLUTELY FREE!

3. Then, if we don't hear from you, every month we'll send you 6 additional novels to read and enjoy. You can return them and owe nothing, but if you decide to keep them, you'll pay only $2.25 per book—a savings of 25¢ each off the cover price.

4. When you subscribe to the Silhouette Reader Service™, you'll also get our newsletter, as well as additional free gifts from time to time.

5. You must be completely satisfied. You may cancel at any time simply by sending us a note or a shipping statement marked "cancel" or by returning any shipment to us at our expense.

You'll look like a million dollars when you wear this elegant necklace! It's a generous 20 inches long and each link is double-soldered for strength and durability.

"ROLL A DOUBLE!"

PLACE LABEL HERE

SCRATCH HERE

?

SEE CLAIM CHART BELOW

215 CIS ACLU
(U-SIL-R-09/91)

YES! I have placed my label from the front cover into the space provided above and scratched off the silver dice. Please rush me the free book(s) and gift(s) that I am entitled to. I understand that I am under no obligation to purchase any books, as explained on the opposite page.

NAME

ADDRESS   APT.

CITY   STATE   ZIP CODE

CLAIM CHART

4 FREE BOOKS PLUS FREE 20" NECKLACE PLUS MYSTERY BONUS GIFT

3 FREE BOOKS PLUS BONUS GIFT

2 FREE BOOKS

CLAIM NO.37-829

SILHOUETTE "NO RISK" GUARANTEE

- You're not required to buy a single book—ever!
- You must be completely satisfied or you may cancel at any time simply by sending us a note or a shipping statement marked "cancel" or by returning any shipment to us at our cost. Either way, you will receive no more books; you'll have no obligation to buy.
- The free book(s) and gift(s) you claimed on this "Roll A Double" offer remain yours to keep no matter what you decide.

If offer card is missing, please write to:
Silhouette Reader Service, 3010 Walden Ave., P.O. Box 1867, Buffalo, N.Y. 14269-1867

Susan couldn't think of anything she'd like better, yet she knew she had to show some self-control. Thatch had made her feel better about the kiss last night, but she still wanted to move slowly with this man. She didn't trust herself to resist him.

"I'm sorry, Thatch," she said, the smile still on her face, even though it was a bit wobbly, "you're assigned a table and I eat with the crew, except on special occasions."

"I thought there were other restaurants available where we could have some privacy," he said, disappointed.

"Yes, there are, but I need to sit with the crew this morning."

"I see," he said, watching as Charles came up behind Susan. The other man touched her with a familiarity that Thatch already detested.

"Susan, are you ready?"

She nodded, then said to Thatch, "I hope I'll see you at the class this afternoon."

Thatch didn't say anything as she left with Charles Masters. His throat was tight and his arms ached. He didn't think he could blame the pain on the exercises.

It had been all he could do not to reach out and embrace Susan Williams—and nearly more than he could do to stand there and watch as Charles led her away, his arm around her waist.

Chapter Six

At breakfast Thatch joined his tablemates for the first time. Initial impressions had him categorizing them in no time, even though he knew he wasn't being fair.

"And who are you?" a flamboyantly dressed gray-haired matron asked as Thatch slid his chair next to hers at the table for eight.

He smiled. "Most people just call me Thatch."

She glared at him as if the information was not at all satisfactory. Thatch felt as if he'd failed an exam.

"We're Mr. and Mrs. Nossam, from Beverly Hills. Mr. Nossam is a retired lawyer," she announced.

"Ah," Thatch said, as if their names and location said it all. In truth, they probably did. *Mr. and Mrs.,* so they wished to be on formal terms, from *Beverly Hills,* so they probably had money, and Mr. was a retired *lawyer,* so there was even more certainty they had money.

Thatch looked down at the menu by his plate.

"And you? What do you do?" Mrs. Nossam wasn't through with him yet.

"Insurance," he said.

Once more Mrs. Nossam seemed hardly impressed, but apparently viewing herself in the role of hostess, she indicated a woman across from Thatch. "Miss Threadlam is in insurance, too. She's a processor. What do you do in insurance, Mr. Thatch?"

Tamping down the urge to tell her to mind her own business, Thatch forced his attention, first to Miss Threadlam, then to Mrs. Nossam.

"I have my own business," he answered, casting his glance back to Miss Threadlam and giving her a smile. "And the name is Thatch—just Thatch."

She grinned. "Lois, please."

"Lois, it is," he said, enjoying her sweet smile and her casual appearance.

"Is your business in L.A.?" Mrs. Nossam persisted.

"Yes."

Mrs. Nossam looked displeased by the one-word response. However, she didn't give up. "The couple beside you, Mr. and Mrs. Layton, are honeymooning. He's a math teacher and she's a history teacher."

"Congratulations," Thatch said sincerely, studying the glowing young couple. Thatch realized he felt a little envious as they both started to speak, then looked at each other adoringly and indicated that the other continue.

Finally Mr. Layton did. "I'm Carl and this is Carolyn," he said, beaming at his wife. "We were married yesterday."

Thatch couldn't help chuckling at the young man's obvious pleasure and embarrassment—rare in this day and age. "I hope you'll be very happy," he said, looking at Carolyn Layton.

In her early twenties, a plain gaunt woman by any measuring stick, she nevertheless was radiant with love and happiness. Carl, with his thick glasses and lean studious look, was her perfect match, and equally infatuated with his wife. Thatch found himself hoping the glow never dulled.

"Mrs. Cloy Azor," Mrs. Nossam continued, guiding Thatch's gaze to an elderly woman decked out in jewels.

"Sheila," the plump woman said. "Cloy was a doctor. He's no longer with us, may he rest in peace."

"A pleasure to meet you," Thatch said, trying to be polite.

"Likewise, I'm sure," the widow said, with equally impersonal politeness.

"And our final tablemate, Mr. Harold Duran," Mrs. Nossam said, indicating a man on the other side of the widow.

He smiled. "Harry," the man said. "And I'm in shoes. I sell them in the mall."

Thatch smiled knowingly as Harry winked, giving the message that he was merely a working man, then glanced at Lois Threadlam.

"Coffee?" Harry asked Thatch, reaching for the steaming silver pot in front of him.

"Yes, please."

Coffee might be just what Thatch needed. When he'd poured himself a cup and taken a sip of the strong eye-opener, a waiter appeared for their orders.

Only half caring what he ate, Thatch sized up the other diners in the room. When his gaze fell on a pretty blonde, he realized what he was really doing was looking for Susan.

He returned his gaze to his tablemates, recalling that Eva had the second meal sitting and wondering whom she would meet. He hoped for her sake she wound up with a more companionable group than he had.

As soon as the thought entered his mind, he was irritated with himself. *Mr. Cynic,* he chastised himself. He didn't know these folks, and he, of all people, had learned you couldn't tell a book by its cover. Mrs. Nossam had annoyed him by taking over, but he knew that someone needed to break the ice.

He recalled Susan's saying that the briefing last night was to serve that purpose, but Thatch hadn't stayed. He'd been too busy ruminating on Susan's many attractions and his lack of attention to the job.

He stared down at his water glass. He knew why he was dissatisfied with his dining companions, and it had nothing to do with them. He'd wanted to spend this time with Susan, and she'd refused him.

"Thatch?"

"I beg your pardon," he said, glancing up to see who had addressed him. It seemed that he was *still* ruminating about Susan Williams!

"I asked what you thought of the trip so far?" Lois Threadlam said.

"It's a lot more than I expected," Thatch said. Boy, was that the truth, he added to himself. Again he pictured Susan. There he went again!

"Have you taken a cruise before?" she asked.

He shook his head. "I don't particularly care for being on the water."

"Oh, a ship is the only way to go," Harry interjected. "This is my third cruise, and I wouldn't vacation any other way."

"Have you been to Mexico?" Lois asked, directing her conversation to Harry.

Thatch relaxed a little, settling back in his chair. The group had found itself. Carl and Carolyn were eagerly murmuring to each other about Acapulco, the Nossams were talking to the doctor's widow about their many travels, Lois and Harry were chatting, and Thatch was left to his musings and observations, one of which was that Harry, the shoe salesman, was taking his third cruise.

After he'd eaten an order of *huevos revueltos con salsa*—scrambled eggs with sauce—and toast, he excused himself.

"See you at lunch, if not before," Lois said.

Thatch nodded. "You bet."

Then he wandered leisurely out of the dining room, his mind racing, his eyes exploring as he went. In the hall, he paused for a moment to make mental notes, then moved to the elevators.

As though guided by an invisible force, he found himself in the gym. Dressed in a body-defining deep yellow leotard, yellow-and-white leg warmers and yellow tennis shoes, Susan was working out to Latin music with more energy and more appeal than any one woman should have.

A few other people were trying to follow along, but Susan wasn't conducting an exercise session, Thatch saw. She was feverishly working out a routine. He didn't see how the others could hope to stay up with her.

Pretending to check out the facilities, Thatch wandered over to the exercise equipment, but all he could see, no matter who was on a machine, was Susan. Since yesterday she'd become the driving force behind everything he did; he couldn't understand it or explain it—or suppress her lovely image.

The moment Susan saw Thatch enter, she remembered she'd promised him a tour. He seemed to be doing fine by himself. She continued her routine for a few more minutes, observing Thatch from the corner of her eye.

Although he was dressed in green shorts and a green-and-red shirt, affecting the look of the archetypal cruise passenger, Susan couldn't help thinking he was anything but. Abruptly he turned and caught her staring, a knack he had that made her suspect the man had second sight.

Thatch grinned in embarrassment. Susan smiled and gave him a little wave. As though the magic of *Mexico Magic* belonged solely to Susan, Thatch found himself lured toward the woman when she turned off the music and patted the perspiration on her forehead with a thick white towel.

"I didn't know if you'd seen me or not when I came in," Thatch said, noticing the other people who were watching the recreational assistant as if to see what she'd do next.

She nodded. "I saw you. I was preparing for my four-o'clock session."

"Will you be conducting that here in the gym?" one of the women asked.

"Yes," Susan said warmly. "I hope all of you will join me then."

"What about the ballroom dancing?" another woman asked.

Susan laughed as she tossed her damp braid over her shoulder. "I love a group that participates. You all are going to be just great! The dance lessons will start at two this afternoon."

"Will we learn any Mexican dances before we get to Mexico?" someone asked.

"I'll start instruction in those tomorrow at two," Susan said, "in plenty of time before we dock at Puerto Vallarta on Thursday. I hope I'll see all of you then, too. And don't forget," she added, "tonight, after the Captain's Dinner, we have our Mexican Musical Extravaganza, where you can preview some of the dances we'll try."

Satisfied, the group trailed off to other parts of the gym.

"Boy, you keep some schedule," Thatch murmured to Susan.

"That's what I'm paid for," she replied cheerfully.

The fact that the data on her revealed she was wealthy pushed relentlessly to the surface of Thatch's mind. He wanted badly to confront her then and there about it, but it was really none of his business.

At least, it wasn't any of his business yet.

"Where's Charles?" he asked.

"He should be conducting a class, either in tennis or racquetball," Susan said. "He handles that part of the recreational activities."

"Does he give dance lessons?" Thatch asked.

"Yes. There are never enough male partners for the women, Thatch. I do hope you'll come to the classes."

Susan Williams was the only woman Thatch wanted to hold in his arms, but he knew the dance class was one more way to interact with people.

"I'm not very good in that area," he said truthfully.

Laughter lit Susan's face. "*That's* the reason you should take lessons!"

"I suppose so," Thatch conceded.

Susan studied his attractive face, wondering which man she was dealing with today—the elusive one, or the lover who'd sent chills up and down her spine last night.

"Shall I show you around?" she offered.

"By all means," he agreed, trying not to stare as she wrapped the towel around her shoulders, the thick terry cloth doing nothing to conceal her beauty.

When she slipped a sweatband off her head, Thatch had the most absurd urge to smooth her wayward bangs. He shoved his hands into his pockets and followed Susan.

"We have a terrific exercise setup," she said.

"That's an understatement," Thatch agreed, having noted nearly every piece of equipment currently on the market, along with floor-to-ceiling mirrors for those who wanted to view their progress, or lack of it.

"The pool is available to passengers at all times."
Susan indicated the large indoor pool with its sparkling blue water. "We also have saunas, whirlpool
baths and three massage rooms, with masseurs and
masseuses available by appointment only, from six-
thirty in the morning to ten-thirty at night. You might
find a massage relaxing, Thatch," she added. "I love
them myself."

A vision of Susan lying nude on a massage table,
perhaps with only a towel draped over her shapely
derriere, prodded Thatch's overactive imagination and
he struggled to erase the tempting image. It was difficult enough seeing her in the provocative leotard.

"This really is incredible," he said. "Can you believe I've never been on a ship before?"

"Is it because the price was prohibitive?" Susan
asked innocently. The package price for an extended
cruise could be expensive.

When she saw the curious expression on Thatch's
face, she realized she was prying again. "Truly, I'm
not fixated on money," she hurried to say, "or people's lack or abundance of it. I know that a cruise is a
luxury for most people. I didn't mean to imply perhaps you couldn't afford it."

Damn! She wished she'd thought before she spoke.
She was so used to price being an issue, especially with
her mother harping on money, or people without it,
that she automatically assumed someone didn't have
the money for a trip when they were reluctant to travel.
She was so enamored with cruises herself that she forgot they weren't everyone's favorite way to vacation.

"Actually I wouldn't pay this kind of money for a trip," Thatch said, wondering again at her preoccupation with money. "I told you I won the trip."

"Yes, you did," she said quickly. "However, that certainly doesn't mean you couldn't afford it, and I didn't mean to imply that you couldn't. What I meant—"

"What *did* you mean?" he interrupted. He really did want to know. He wanted to understand this woman, and why they kept coming back to the subject of money.

Susan sighed. "What is it about us, Thatch," she murmured, "that causes us to speak to each other so suspiciously, with such doubt and question in our voices, or causes us to always be trying to explain away some innocent remark? Are you constantly on edge, or do I set you off?"

He tightened his fists in his pockets. He could come up with several answers to her questions. He was naturally suspicious, and she seemed naturally nosy. She was a member of the staff, and he was a spy. The combination didn't work to best advantage for them.

He sighed. "I don't know. I think the problem is that I'm a private person and you always seem to be..."

"Prying?" she filled in for him. Her gaze held his. "I don't mean to, Thatch. You misread me, and that makes me seem nosier than I am. I *like* people, I'm interested in them, I try to learn something about them, to bring them out of themselves, to make them more comfortable. If you have something to hide, that's your business. I'm not trying to find out anything you don't want to tell me."

He shook his head and looked away, thinking once more what a great private detective this woman would be. *He* was the one who should be prying, to use her term, asking questions, learning things. But he couldn't seem to where she was concerned.

He looked into those appealing brown eyes, and he wanted to confess everything he was thinking, everything he'd ever thought, everything he might think. He had taken his hands out of his pockets and embraced Susan's shoulders before he was brought back to his senses by the soft feel of her skin.

Hell! he thought, startled at finding himself on the other side of the questions, wanting to give her all the answers so that she could understand this tension between them.

He reluctantly let his hands slide down her arms. "It's me, not you, Susan," he said simply. "I can't open up the way you do, and I guess I resent your questions."

Hell! There he went again, trying to tell her about himself.

Susan didn't look away. "I can't decide," she murmured as much to herself as to him, "if you like me or not, Thatch, if you resent me, or want to get to know me, if I'm throwing myself at you, or you're chasing me."

"I can answer some of those questions," he said in an equally musing voice. "I like you, but I don't know you. You were right that we're moving way too fast here."

"I see," she said. He was echoing her words, and that was not at all what she wanted to hear. Yes, they *were* moving too fast. Yes, he'd scared her off with his intimate caresses last night.

But she wanted more. They had less than three weeks to get to know each other. And she wondered if a lifetime would be enough.

"I'd better let you get back to work," Thatch said.

He couldn't stand here with this woman and not touch her, not talk to her. It simply wasn't in him not to reach out to her, mentally and physically. The only cure was distance. Absence may or may not make the heart grow fonder, but it sure prevented vocal and visual contact.

As he turned away, Susan asked, "Are you coming to the dance classes, Thatch?"

"Yes."

Watching as he went out the door, Susan wondered if he really would show up. She wanted him to, much more than was wise.

When Thatch closed the door, he found himself thinking that wild horses couldn't keep him away from Susan Williams. And he wondered how he could knowingly continue heedlessly and headlong into her life.

And what was he going to do about it?

Chapter Seven

Thatch spent the intervening hours between the time he'd seen Susan in the gym and two o'clock doing a little sleuthing here and there on the ship, chatting with other passengers and staff, in general getting a feel for the people on board. He had a drink on the Fiesta Deck with the sun-worshipers, ambled about in the casino, noting the heavy gamblers, and managed to get himself conveniently lost on the Glorioso Deck, where many of the crew were housed.

He had already made it a point to be friendly with his cabin boy, Miguel, so while he was on the Glorioso Deck, he chatted with the young man for a few minutes and met more of the employees. The task of putting names with data seemed monumental, but fortunately Thatch had a retentive memory.

At least, that was true when he wasn't thinking of Susan Williams—which he was doing most of the time. He surprised himself by keeping an eye on his watch, eagerly awaiting the time the dance lessons would begin.

No matter how he tried to reason with himself, he came to the same conclusion about Susan. She really was Miss Susy Sunshine, a sunbeam, an unexpected ray of brightness, a highlight in his life, someone who stirred faded sweet dreams, dreams lingering at the edges of his mind, dreams he'd thought he no longer had.

And that scared him.

Susan was clearly unprepared for Thatch to be the first person to show up for dance instruction. She was studying her image in the mirror when Thatch walked in.

She had changed clothes again, this time to a lovely golden dress cinched at the waist with a full skirt that flared out gracefully. She wore three-inch heels in the same shade of gold, and what they did for her legs was enough to make a man's heart stop.

"Am I early?" Thatch asked, hoping his voice didn't betray him as he soaked up the sight of Susan. She'd left her hair down, and the thick waves fell past her shoulders in an enchanting golden cascade.

She laughed lightly as she caught his reflection in the mirror. She realized that she had been waiting anxiously for him to come, afraid he wouldn't show up at all. The fact that he was early only excited her more.

"Yes, you are," she said.

He grinned. "Good. I didn't want to humiliate myself in front of the others by asking you for a couple of private lessons."

Susan hesitated, knowing that she shouldn't dance with him alone. But, oh, how she wanted to! She longed for him to touch her again. And what harm could a dance or two do? The others would be along soon.

"Since you're here early, maybe we can work something out," she said. "We'll try a few steps now, if you'd like."

"Yes, I would," he said, willing to accept any conditions.

After switching on the tape deck, Susan held out her arms. "We'll begin with a basic waltz," she said, aware of the husky sound in her voice as she never had been before. It was almost as if she were struggling to catch her breath. The thought of being in Thatch's arms made her heart beat ridiculously fast.

"All right." He took her hand in his and put his arm around her waist. "Like this?" he murmured.

Speechless, Susan nodded and looked down at her feet. Her pulse was pounding in her ears so loudly she could hardly hear the music. She wanted to draw in a long, slow steadying breath and force her body to calm down, but she was afraid that would be all too revealing. She was embarrassed enough already to think that Thatch could feel her quivering.

Thatch watched her demonstrate the steps they would do, then he imitated them.

"Great!" Susan said. "Let's try it together."

When Thatch drew her more closely to him and moved with her to the music, Susan felt as if her breath had been completely stolen away. In her heels, she molded to his body perfectly, breast to chest, hip

off the music. Then she motioned the others forward so that she could begin instruction.

When Charles emerged from the midst of the crowd, Susan could see that he was irritated and it didn't take a crystal ball to know why. Determined not to battle with him in front of the passengers, she gave him a big smile, then spoke.

"Ladies, we're doubly lucky today! We have another wonderful dancing partner. He is, of course, Charles Masters, our recreational director."

Thatch thought Charles smiled smugly at him, though perhaps it was his imagination. He glanced around, seeing the rest of the group for the first time.

Apparently ballroom dancing was a popular cruise pastime, for there were many older couples, as well as younger ones, and several unescorted women, along with a few single men.

Eva was there. So was Sir Roger Nester. Thatch's mind started spinning with suspicions.

Sir Roger was a fake if ever he'd seen one. He was a repeat passenger, and he was impoverished, according to the information Thatch had been able to find on him. For all the above, Thatch placed him at the top of his list of possible thieves. But, of course, he'd only begun the list.

The minute Susan started the music again, a woman clasped Thatch's hand, interrupting his speculation.

"Be my partner?" she coaxed coyly.

Thatch couldn't help noticing she was a stunningly attractive brunette, about five-foot-five, with huge brown eyes. Brown eyes almost as pretty as Susan Williams's. Almost, but not quite.

"All right," Susan said, drawing everyone's attention back to her. "Charles and I will demonstrate each dance. If you have any questions, or need extra help, don't hesitate to tell us."

Thatch forgot about the woman at his side as he watched Charles take Susan in his arms with a familiarity that caused a flare of jealousy in the pit of Thatch's stomach. He wanted to be the one holding her, smiling at her, leading her gracefully around the floor. Well, maybe not so gracefully as Charles, but he did want to be with her.

"Let's try it," the brunette urged, squeezing Thatch's hand.

He looked down at her. He'd say one thing for the women on this boat—they didn't lack initiative.

Giving in to her plea, he took her in his arms and began to perform the same steps Susan had shown him earlier. He instantly stepped on the woman's left foot, then promptly on the right when he tried to get off the left.

"I'm sorry," he apologized profusely, his face flushing. He really never had been able to dance. Dancing with Susan had been magic, but now his feet were back on the floor, or worse, on his partner's.

"It's okay," she said, though there was a puzzled expression on her attractive face.

"I can't dance," Thatch said, "no matter what you think if you watched me and the instructor. It was either her skill, or pure illusion."

The brunette laughed. "It's okay, really. I've danced with worse, and at least I have a good-looking man in my arms."

She gestured toward several women who had no one to dance with. "They can't wait for you to step on their feet."

Thatch's laughter drew Susan's gaze to his face. Their eyes met briefly. She'd seen him stumble on his partner's feet and had been thoroughly puzzled. Apparently Thatch was comfortable with her, and consequently able to dance well. The man in the brunette's arms was clearly the bashful boy coming to the surface again.

As Charles skillfully spun her around, Susan smiled encouragingly at Thatch, even though she was secretly pleased he wasn't dancing as well with his new partner as he had with her. The moment had been so rare, so special. It formed a memory she would take home with her.

At the startling reminder that memories might be all she would ever have of Thatch, her spirits sank. It took all her concentration to smile pleasantly and pretend to be having the time of her life in Charles's arms.

Seeing Susan's radiant smile directed at him, Thatch relaxed a little and began to move more easily with his partner. She wasn't the one he wanted, but Susan was only a little distance from him; he could watch her to his heart's content.

Unexpectedly another couple bumped into Thatch, causing him to stagger slightly against the brunette. He looked over his shoulder to see that Eva and Sir Roger were the couple.

"Sorry, old chap," the man said.

"It was my fault," Eva insisted politely, graciously. "I'm afraid I'm rusty. I haven't danced in years." A dreamy look stole over her face. "Oh, how my late husband and I enjoyed it!"

Thatch happened to know Eva had never been married. Sir Roger immediately began to subtly question her about her dear departed mate. Not at all surprised, Thatch eavesdropped interestedly as the questions predictably came to what line of work Eva's late husband had been in.

He almost choked when the smiling, angelic-looking, gray-haired woman answered, "He was a diamond buyer. We traveled all over the world, especially Africa, of course."

Thatch recovered only to nervously await Eva's answer when Sir Roger, who'd evidently been to Africa, asked direct and detailed questions. Thatch should have known he had no need to worry. As Eva expertly fielded the man's questions, Thatch found a space on the dance floor that was less crowded.

He was immediately tapped on the shoulder by a woman who'd been standing on the fringe of the floor. He glanced at the brunette in his arms.

She shrugged. "I told you they couldn't wait for you to trip on their toes." Smiling, she relinquished him.

Thatch wondered if she wasn't happy to escape his clumsy dancing, but he didn't have time to ponder the question. A series of women came in and out of his arms as the hour-long dance session, during which three more dances were introduced, continued.

Although it was an excellent opportunity for Thatch to get to know the women a bit, he told himself by the time the lessons ended that he was going to need a nap between them and the Captain's Dinner. He was more inept with each new dance, partly because every time he watched Charles and Susan together, he forgot to pay attention. His partners, though, didn't seem to notice.

Thatch was more than glad when Charles ended the dance session with a round of applause for all those participating. Thatch automatically searched for Susan. She and Charles had danced with other partners throughout the hour, but Thatch hadn't been lucky enough to have Susan in his arms again.

When he saw that Susan and Charles were gathering up the tapes and the tape deck, their muted voices sharp, their eyes announcing—at least to anyone observant enough to notice—that they were angry with each other, Thatch sighed. Susan might not consider the two of them an item, but he believed Charles did. He was trying to decide whether to go over to them when they went out of the room.

Thatch was left to his own devices. A nap was apparently his only choice. Susan was going somewhere with her boss.

A frown on his face, Thatch stared after the couple a moment longer, as if he could draw Susan back to him by the sheer force of his desire. After a bit, he shoved his hands into his pockets and left the room, irrationally disappointed because he hadn't been able to speak with Susan again.

Immediately he crashed into a warm female body. "Sorry," he murmured, startled. He didn't recall ever being this bumbling in his life!

"Oh, it's you," Merry Lou Addison said. "Are the dance lessons over?"

Thatch nodded, glad this woman had missed them. It would have been his bad luck to have her again start suggesting she knew him.

"Was a British gentleman with a handlebar mustache there, do you know?" Merry Lou asked.

"I believe he was," Thatch said.

Merry Lou glanced at her watch. "I must have been right about the time. I thought the session began at two, but Sir Roger believed it started at three, that there had been a scheduling change."

Thatch tried not to show his surprise at the devious old gentleman. Thatch would stake his reputation Roger had lied intentionally to get rid of Merry Lou and spend time with Eva.

"Pardon me," Merry Lou said, brushing past Thatch, "maybe he's still in there."

Although grateful not to be the focus of Merry Lou's attention, Thatch was glad he'd seen Roger and Eva leave. It was too early for a confrontation of any kind.

To Susan's disappointment, she'd felt obligated to hear Charles out, away from the others. She'd really wanted to talk with Thatch after the dance session.

"Do you have more problems, Charles?" she snapped, turning to her boss. "Do you want me to walk the plank for imagined transgressions?"

"What I want you to do," he returned equally sharply, "is remember that you're here to do a job, not let a single passenger usurp your time while others attending classes wait as you float around the floor like a love-struck teenager."

Susan sucked in her breath. "I did *not* do that! The others hadn't arrived when Thatch and I began to dance." She didn't dare deny the love-struck part, because she was afraid she would be lying if she did.

"When you *began* to dance, yes!" he flung at her. "But," he said, stabbing a finger at her, "I watched you dance two dances with him while the other students waited."

"They didn't complain," she retorted. "In fact, they seemed to enjoy it. They clapped."

"I think, my dear," he said sarcastically, "they were relieved to see that the two of you weren't actually stuck together, as appeared to be the case."

In spite of herself, Susan blushed. It was also true that she hadn't felt she could get close enough to Thatch. She had pressed against him as tightly as she could.

"If you can manage," Charles said, his eyes flashing, perhaps we'd better look over the list of passengers going ashore at Puerto Vallarta. Or do you have other plans?"

"No, of course not," she murmured.

She hadn't made any plans with Thatch, even though she'd hoped to. Dutifully, for it was her duty to be with Charles, she did as he ordered.

Thatch was amazed he was able to nap, even though last night's rest had been unsatisfactory to say the least. When he woke up, it was time to dress for the Captain's Dinner.

Stretching, he noticed the stiffness in his muscles from the unfamiliar activity of dancing. As he lay in bed savoring the memory of Susan gliding about the dance floor with him, he wondered if he would see her at dinner.

After Thatch had chosen his gray suit and a blue shirt over his navy suit and a white shirt, he dressed hurriedly, then left the room. He was running a bit late. Most of the halls were clear of people and the elevators were empty.

As he entered the dining room, he saw why. The Captain's Dinner was obviously a big deal. People were dressed to the nines, diamonds and rubies accenting their outfits. Thatch felt like a hobo in his three-year-old suit, but there was nothing to do except join the others.

Mrs. Nossam assessed him critically as he sat down. After a brief nod, she continued her discussion with Sheila Azor about who was seated at the place of honor with the captain. Thatch's gaze was drawn to the long table where the uniformed man sat.

He was surprised to see Susan and Charles side by side among the many diners—surprised and jealous. He allowed himself only a quick survey of Susan, deciding that she was impossibly beautiful in a long white gown, her hair piled on top of her head. He could see that the dress had a split from the thigh down, causing it to fall away from one long pretty leg.

Forcing his gaze away, he distracted himself with the less than beautiful females at his own table. "Ladies," he said, "you all look gorgeous tonight."

Even Mrs. Nossam smiled at the compliment. "Why, thank you, Thatch," she gushed. "Mr. Nossam was growing angry with me because I couldn't decide which gown to wear. I'm glad I selected this one. I think white suits me much better than beige."

Thatch hadn't even noticed the woman was wearing white, but he was pleased to have finally done something right with her. She was calling him Thatch.

Still, despite all his good intentions, the mention of the white dress automatically sent his gaze back across the room to the captain's table. Susan was laughing at something someone said.

Thatch returned his attention to Mrs. Nossam, though he could hardly wait for the dinner to be over. He hoped Susan wouldn't leave with Charles. He wanted to see her alone tonight. He didn't even bother to acknowledge the warnings going off inside his brain about how foolish he was being.

He'd already accepted the fact that he'd succumbed to Miss Susy Sunshine's charms. He'd known when he danced with her in the studio that he was in this for the long haul, regardless of the results. Whatever happened, he was resigned to take it like a man and handle it the best he could.

He just hoped his surrender to Susan Williams didn't cost him more than he could afford to pay. Or worse—cost someone else.

To Thatch's chagrin, his determination to see Susan when dinner was over proved futile. The mass of people milled about, chatting with each other, forming traffic jams and pairing up to go to the Mexican Musical Extravaganza. By the time Thatch reached the captain's table, it was empty.

His search of the Fiesta Deck only reminded him of how many lovers were on board, and the knowledge didn't help any. He combed several other decks, looking in shops and stores, and went to all the lounges, but Susan wasn't there. He even called her room, but to no avail.

It wasn't until he saw Eva and Roger sharing a glass of wine in an outdoor café that he was reminded he wasn't on board for his health or the love of a beautiful woman. He wasn't being fair to Eva, he told himself, surreptitiously studying the older couple.

Eva didn't seem to care or know; she was engrossed in what Roger was telling her. Thatch stiffened his back and his resolve. Someone had to get on with the job. *He* had to get on with it. Supposedly Eva was doing her part, even though that didn't appear to be the case at this particular time.

At least she was with a viable suspect. He was hunting for Susan! It wasn't until he returned to his room that he found her, and that was in his dreams.

The next morning, as Susan conducted the aquatic exercises on the Fiesta Deck, she scanned the students for some sign of Thatch. He was nowhere to be seen. While she went about her duties the rest of the morning, she kept a lookout for him. She remained disappointed as her mind whirled with pictures and questions about Thatch.

After Charles had excused her the previous night, she'd haunted the ship, searching for Thatch to no avail, even going so far as to wait in the lounge where they'd shared a drink. He was nowhere to be found, and she wouldn't let herself ring his room.

Disgusted, she'd finally gone to bed, but that hadn't stopped the thoughts of him. She'd had some silly notion that he would try to see her. She'd imagined that they'd shared something special there on the studio dance floor.

What had gone wrong since they'd held each other? She had been sure he'd felt at least a little of what she'd felt then. His heartbeat had been as erratic as her own when they danced.

Had that only been nervousness on his part? He'd told her he couldn't dance, and she'd questioned her own sanity after she'd seen him in the arms of other women. He *had* been very awkward then, and she'd egotistically attributed his refined dancing to her finesse—or worse, his interest in her.

Sighing, she tried to put thoughts of Thatch aside. It seemed an impossible task. When it was almost time for the Latin dance lessons, she hurried to the studio early, hoping for a repeat of yesterday.

There were a few women in the room when she arrived, but no Thatch. Her heart began sinking as she readied the music and glanced over her shoulder to see who was attending the session. There were plenty of passengers, but not the man Susan wanted to see.

She'd almost given up on him when Charles joined her at the front of the room to help her teach. "These are fun dances," she was telling the participants when Thatch strolled into the room.

"Now, pay attention," Susan cautioned the students, though she herself could hardly think of anything but Thatch. "We'll be in Puerto Vallarta tomorrow. You may want to try out your new dancing skills."

Thatch was paying close attention, though he didn't give a hoot about trying out his dance skills. He was waiting for the opportunity to speak with Susan alone. He was hardly aware of the exotic beat of the music, or the giggles and laughter of the others as they participated in a variety of folk dances.

After the hour had dragged interminably, Charles finally shut off the music. Thatch didn't wait around this time. All during the dance lessons, he hadn't had a single chance to talk with Susan.

"Susan!" he called, crossing the floor.

She and Charles both turned. "How about that shopping expedition in Puerto Vallarta you and I talked about?" he asked. "Are you going to help me bargain with the merchants?"

Looking confused for a moment, Susan swallowed hard and forced a smile to her lips. Thatch had said he wasn't much for shopping, but she didn't care. She only wanted to be with him.

"Yes, of course."

He lightly brushed her fingers with his own. "Thanks."

"No problem," she said, her heart hammering.

Thatch turned away, wishing he didn't have to go, wishing he could ask Susan to spend the rest of the afternoon with him, however he could practically feel Charles's hostility. He didn't want to push his luck.

Or Susan's.

Shoving his hands into his pockets, he began to whistle softly to himself as he walked away.

He spun around when Merry Lou caught up with him. "Have you seen Sir Roger anywhere today?"

Thatch shook his head. In fact, he hadn't. He had a rendezvous with Eva later. Although he'd half expected her and Roger to be at the Latin dance lessons, they hadn't come.

Merry Lou had been there, but as long as she hadn't bothered him, Thatch'd figured live and let live.

"That lying scoundrel!" she muttered bitterly. "He promised he'd meet me here, and he never turned up."

"Sorry," Thatch said, disengaging his arm from her fingers. "I don't know anything about the gentleman."

"He can't fool me," Merry Lou said with venom. "I know what he's up to. I've met his kind everywhere I've traveled, and I've traveled plenty!"

Indeed! Thatch thought to himself, the idea sending a spurt of adrenaline through him. He didn't want to indulge Merry Lou, or encourage her, yet he felt he had to pursue the topic—but discreetly.

"What's the matter?" he asked solicitously. "What are you talking about? Has the man done you some kind of wrong?"

"Ha!" Merry Lou said bitterly. "Me? No, in fact, I'm the lucky one. It's that stupid widow who's going to be done wrong."

"Pardon me?" Thatch said, all his senses on alert. "Is someone in trouble?"

"Oh, never mind," Merry Lou said, disgust in her voice.

"Wait, Mrs.—"

"I said never mind!" she repeated with all the righteous indignation of a woman scorned.

Thatch had seen that behavior too many times in his line of work. His mind whirling, he watched the voluptuous blonde stalk off, every line of her body revealing her distress.

Thatch definitely was going to have to talk with Eva tonight!

Chapter Eight

When Thatch met Eva on the top deck, she ignored him completely, letting him know by a code they had worked out in advance that she had everything under control.

Thatch wondered. He wasn't at all satisfied, yet he knew there was nothing to do. Until some jewelry was stolen, surveillance and awareness were his only options. He would have more of a chance to speak with Eva in Puerto Vallarta.

"Hell!" he muttered in irritation. Susan would be with him. How stupid could one man be? He'd been so eager to see her away from the ship, away from Charles and the other passengers, that he'd behaved unwisely.

He sighed. He really was giving this job less than his best, but it wasn't the end of the world—or the case—

yet. He'd work out something inventive. Presuming, of course, that the thief struck.

Although the ship was a floating hotel, with all those who wished to remain on board doing so, the passengers had the option of spending the night in the Mexican coastal town to get the maximum benefit from the time there.

Thatch planned to stay over. He had phone calls to make and possibilities to follow through on that he didn't want anyone to know about. He also *had* to talk to Eva.

His mind in turmoil, he returned to his room and tried to get some sleep. The night seemed endless, but eventually exhaustion overtook him.

Susan was awake well before the ship's bell announced their arrival in Puerto Vallarta. The once-isolated fishing village had become one of the country's most popular resorts. It was still a favorite of hers, with its hillside houses and condos, its cobblestone streets and lovely beaches.

However, she knew that what she was really looking forward to was spending time with Thatch. She wanted to get to know him without all the distractions of the ship. The onshore shopping excursion was only an excuse to be with him.

Fortunately most of the ship's passengers were familiar with the port and had no need of Charles and Susan's services. Charles had agreed to guide a handful of women, and although he'd balked at Susan's refusal to join him, both of them knew her presence wasn't essential.

Dressed in yellow slacks and a yellow-and-white T-shirt, her hair in its customary braid, Susan was helping other crew members direct the first of the passengers off the ship when she saw Thatch.

"Ready?" he asked, walking up to stand beside her.

Her gaze swept over him. He was dressed in blue jeans and a T-shirt, which surprised her. He looked more boldly male than ever—almost predatory, in fact. Susan couldn't help thinking that he looked like a male animal on the prowl—cool, collected and concentrating on an objective. She shivered as she realized there was no sign at all of the bashful boy in him now.

"Will you wait just a moment?" she asked, her tone husky with an elementary awareness of him. "Charles has already gone ahead with a group, and I need to stay a little longer to see that the disembarking goes smoothly."

She needed to stay a little longer, too, to get used to the sight of Thatch!

"Fine," he said, smiling as his gaze encompassed her from golden braid to yellow sneakers. "Do you like yellow?" he asked, the question seemingly unnecessary since she constantly wore the color.

"Actually I do," she said with a broad smile, exposing those dimples Thatch loved, "but any combination of yellow, brown and white is also the ship uniform."

Thatch slapped his forehead with the palm of his hand. "My word! Of course," he said. "How singularly lacking in observation can one man be?"

Especially an investigator, he added to himself. The fact that most of the others wore brown was no excuse either. Susan simply looked so radiant in yellow that he hadn't thought beyond that.

Suddenly Merry Lou turned up. Thatch couldn't believe it. Out of all the people on the ship, how did she manage to appear where he was so often? He was beginning to think the woman was tailing him. She was really starting to grate on his nerves.

"Have you seen Sir Roger Nester?" she asked Susan, ignoring Thatch, for which he was unprepared though extremely grateful.

Susan shook her head. "No, I haven't. Did you try his room?"

"Yes—and no one answered." Merry Lou lowered her voice. "Have you seen Eva Adkins? Has she left the ship?"

"Eva's the tall gray-haired lady in her fifties or sixties, isn't she?" Susan asked, frowning slightly as she tried to sort through the passengers in her mind.

Thatch pretended to study the disembarking people. He saw Eva—without Roger—but of course he kept silent.

Susan scanned the crowd, then gestured toward Eva. "Isn't that the woman?"

Looking like the cat who'd swallowed the canary, Merry Lou grinned. "Yes, it is indeed. Without Roger."

"Do you want to try and catch up with her?" Susan asked helpfully.

The woman shook her head. "I don't think so. I'll just let her go on alone. I have a headache. I think I'll go back to my room and lie down."

Thatch's mind was already spinning. Why was Merry Lou intentionally letting Susan think she and

Eva were friendly? Thatch had noticed that Merry Lou had cultivated the friendship of some elderly single women, but not Eva.

So Sir Roger was staying aboard! If Thatch's suspicions proved correct, Merry Lou would put a crimp in Sir Roger's plans, if indeed he had any, and if Merry Lou located him.

"I think I can leave now," Susan said, stirring Thatch from his thoughts.

"Great." He tried to slow his whirling mind. What he was thinking was all speculation, but Sir Roger's staying on ship did add fuel to the fire....

The day spent in Puerto Vallarta was one of fun and relaxation for Thatch and Susan. In the Mexican town, under the bright sun, they both let their guards down a little, laughing and shopping, Thatch spending money for things he didn't need just so he could watch Susan try to bargain with the vendors.

He did, at Susan's suggestion, buy a Mexican costume for the Christmas Eve party. Susan had explained that while people wore any and everything, many of the passengers, and all of the staff, dressed in Mexican clothing for the party, which was *the* event of the trip.

It amused him to hear Susan with her Southern drawl, speaking with the clothing-store owner in halting half-Spanish. He was tempted to converse with the man himself, until, smiling in amusement, the owner announced that he spoke adequate English and had only wanted to hear Susan's Southern-Spanish.

All three of them were laughing by the time Susan and Thatch, who'd talked the shop owner into holding on to their many purchases until closing time, departed for the beach. There they had a tasty impromptu feast of roasted fish-on-a-stick.

Later, they went to Mismaloya Beach, which was the setting for the movie *Night of the Iguana*. Upon their return, they picked up their packages from the store and headed for an exclusive restaurant for a lobster dinner.

To their surprise, Charles was there. He was seated at a long table overlooking the water with several female passengers, including Eva.

"Oh," Susan murmured, her thoughts of a romantic evening at one of the quiet little tables in back evaporating, "perhaps we should join them, Thatch." Her expression told him it wasn't what she would have chosen to do, but what she felt obligated to do. "We don't want to appear rude. I *am* part of the crew, and Charles is working."

Thatch looked, and felt, as disappointed as Susan, although actually this was a blessing in disguise. One look at Eva chatting animatedly prompted Thatch to remember that he wasn't on this trip for a romantic interlude with Susan.

Eva was working—doing precisely what *he* was supposed to do. Eva had cleverly seated herself next to Charles and was commanding his full attention.

The dinner would give Thatch a chance to visibly establish more than a nodding acquaintance with Eva. Later on, he would be able to speak with her more freely, without attracting attention.

"I think it's a good idea to join them," Thatch said. "But first, Susan," he murmured, "I want to tell you how much I enjoyed our day. I haven't relaxed that completely in so long that I don't remember the last time."

"I had a lovely time, Thatch," she said, looking into his blue eyes. "The day was a very special one for me, too."

Thatch was already beginning to regret his decision to join the others at dinner, even though he knew it was the only practical thing to do. "Don't tell me it was in the line of duty," he said half-jokingly.

Susan looked stricken for a moment. "Trust me, Thatch," she said solemnly, "it was anything but in the line of duty. In fact, it was so far away from it that I'm ashamed of neglecting the other passengers. That's why I think we should sit with them."

Thatch took her hand in his and lightly squeezed her fingers. "Agreed," he said.

Still, for a moment, he couldn't look away from her. Something was happening between them, something he didn't want to face, but would have to sooner or later. He was very much afraid that he was falling for this woman, this blonde, who moved him like no other, who caused the world to stop and to spin at the same time, as impossible as that seemed.

"Susan! Over here!" Charles's sharp voice intruded just in time. Thatch was losing himself in Susan's velvet-brown eyes.

Smiling, Susan exclaimed, "Charles! Ladies! How nice to see you."

Thatch felt as if his feet were weighted with lead as he and Susan joined the table full of chattering passengers, each eager to tell her tale of the exciting time she'd had in Puerto Vallarta.

Eva, pretending to know Thatch only from the ship, chatted with him, using their long-established code to insinuate that perhaps Charles might be worth investigating.

Thatch wasn't surprised. He'd considered the man himself. He felt guilty, though, because Eva seemed to be doing all the work on this case. On the other hand, he wouldn't exchange a moment of his time with Susan for any reason in the world, even loyalty to the job. He wanted this case solved as much as anyone, but his whole world seemed to be shifting with the sea on which *Mexico Magic* sailed. He would juggle the opposing factors as well as he could, though under no circumstances would he stop seeing Susan.

When the meal ended, Thatch was unhappy to learn that Susan was returning to the ship with Charles and the women, including Eva. Yet, he knew it was for the best. Clearly Eva was returning to do her job; he should, as well. She wanted to see if anything had happened on board—particularly with Roger Nester— while she was away.

Thatch had managed to mention that Merry Lou had asked Susan about Eva, and then stayed aboard with a headache. Eva Adkins, the Gray Ghost, was astute enough to read between the lines, Thatch knew.

When Thatch returned to the ship the next morning, he'd learned little more than he'd known the night before. He spent time making work-related phone calls and thinking of Susan, both to no avail.

He was glad when the ship departed for Manzanillo. Nothing had occurred out of the ordinary during the Puerto Vallarta layover, and Thatch was beginning to wonder if he was on a wild-goose chase, searching for a thief who might not even be on board.

However, instinct told him jewels would surely be stolen on this cruise, just as they had on the last three. The problem, he reminded himself, was that in the process of waiting for jewels to be stolen, Susan Williams was stealing his heart!

Manzanillo turned out to be a city of narrow, crowded streets that fulfilled all the fantasies of the tropical coast of Mexico. The jungle vegetation was beautifully colored, and the beaches at Santiago Bay and Las Hadas Cove flaunted yellow sand streaked with black.

Many passengers stayed overnight, but Thatch returned to the ship, taking time to do more sleuthing, and, he'd hoped, to spend time with Susan. She, however, spent the night in town. Thatch, left to his work, resignedly told himself it was about time he concentrated on the job at hand.

The trip to Acapulco was idyllic, as *Mexico Magic* lived up to its name, wrapping passengers and crew alike in a golden haze of pleasure that seemed to remove them from the real world, fulfilling any and every fantasy of even the most travel-weary.

The Christmas Eve party was scheduled for the night before the arrival in Acapulco, and everyone was in high spirits. Every scrap of paper on the ship had been confiscated for wrapping gifts purchased in Puerto Vallarta and Manzanillo for newfound friends and old favorites. Although Thatch had thought he was being original sneaking gifts for Susan and Eva aboard *Magic,* it seemed that many people had secreted presents away.

Thatch was struck by the contagious joy and good humor that circulated throughout the ship. It was almost, he told himself, as if it really was possible to have goodwill among men. He wanted to believe in peace and brotherhood and all those noble things. He wanted to believe in love—because he was very much afraid he was falling in love with Susan Williams.

Susan was all aflutter December twenty-fourth as she dressed for the party. This was the gala, the big event aboard *Magic,* and if past experience was any indication, it would be a splendid occasion indeed.

The ballroom had been decorated festively with colorful detail; the mariachi band, as well as a contemporary American band, had practiced Christmas songs all day, the music ringing out over the ship's loudspeakers; and the cooks had been in the kitchen for hours.

All the preparations were intended to heighten the anticipation of the evening, although Susan didn't think there was a soul on the ship who wasn't already keen to get the evening in motion. She certainly was.

She hadn't found an opportunity to spend time alone with Thatch, even though he had attended exercise classes and she'd passed him coming and going on the different decks. She couldn't wait for eight o'clock to come.

Because she'd helped Thatch select his costume, she knew that he was dressing as a matador, in a resplendent traditional suit, complete with tights, slippers and the bullfighter's hat; however, he'd refused to let her see him when he tried the outfit on.

In retaliation, she hadn't told him how she planned to dress, but now, as she assessed herself in the mirror, she was eager to know what Thatch thought of her costume.

To complement his, she'd dressed as a Mexican folk dancer in a stunning outfit of red and gold, her full-sequined dress ankle-length, her gold high heels visible beneath it. The bodice was peasant-style, low cut with blousy short sleeves edged in gold ribbing. She'd braided her hair and interwoven it with red-and-gold ribbons.

She felt... lovely! And she prayed Thatch would think she was. Too anxious to wait for eight o'clock, she arrived early under the pretext of seeing how everything was coming along.

The room was magnificently decorated with party favors, balloons, colorful streamers and piñatas of every shape and size. The food was a sumptuous array of Mexican fare, from tortillas and tamales to flan de piña, and American favorites, from shrimp cocktails to banana puddings. Every kind of beverage imaginable was lined up at the bars.

"Well, *señorita?*" the head chef said, gazing at the buffet. "What do you think?"

"It looks absolutely *perfecto!*" Susan said, making a circle with her thumb and forefinger. "Beautiful!"

"And so are you," a low male voice said behind them.

Susan spun around, her full skirt swirling about her ankles as she looked at the handsome matador leaning against the opened glass door. Sucking in her breath, she scanned Thatch from head to toe.

In the body-molding suit, he was disturbingly masculine. A matador's costume was designed skintight so that its wearer didn't risk the danger of the bull catching its horn on even the slightest loose piece of cloth. Susan didn't think there was a muscle on Thatch's body that wasn't defined in the brilliant gold-and-silver suit.

Smiling indulgently at the couple, the chef busied himself with finishing touches while Thatch strolled lazily across the room to the pretty *señorita* in the sparkling dress.

"Let's steal a horse and ride off into the sunset," he murmured.

Heavens above! Susan thought. She'd like nothing better, though of course she couldn't do that. And as tempting as it was to have Thatch all to herself, she wanted him to experience the wonder of Christmas on the Mexican Riviera aboard the *Magic*.

"I think matadors fight bulls," she said, trying to control her husky voice. "They don't ride the horses. And, anyway, unless the horse is a Pegasus, I don't think he can make it to shore."

Thatch laughed deeply. "Some romantic you are, Susan Williams! Where's your imagination?"

Although Susan only smiled, she could have told Thatch where her imagination was. It had been running wild ever since she'd first seen him, and it was leashed now by only the loosest of reins. She wanted to tell him that she was even more of a romantic than she'd ever imagined.

For the first time since she'd been hired as a recreational assistant, she was really in dereliction of her duties, as Charles had implied. And she couldn't make herself feel more than a little guilty.

She realized that she'd become disillusioned with men and marriage when her mother shoved every single rich male in the world at her. It had taken someone like Thatch—an unexpected total stranger—to sweep her off her feet and make her not care what happened tomorrow. She was looking forward to this night with him, and the devil take the future!

"Oh, I think I have a tiny bit of romance in my bones," she said lightly, "but we can't spoil all this atmosphere and hard work by running off into the black night." She gestured at the decorations and food. "Look how lovely all this is."

Thatch nodded and smiled without ever looking away from her. "I can see how lovely. In fact, I don't think I've ever seen anything lovelier."

When Susan met his burning gaze, she felt weak and dizzy. She had heard about all the altered states love was supposed to cause, but she'd always believed they were exaggerated. Now she thought they must be understated if she was any example of what happened. She wanted to wrap her arms around Thatch and hold on—forever.

"Susan!"

She was snatched from what seemed to be a single step away from eternity. Staring into Thatch's sea-blue eyes, she'd felt as internally tossed about as if she were really riding waves on the ocean, on a trip from which there was no return. And she hadn't wanted to return.

Charles's gaze swept over her appreciatively, dismissed Thatch, then settled on Susan again. "What do you think?"

Think? she wondered. She thought nothing in the world existed except Thatch. She thought nothing mattered except him and her. She thought the rest of the world was an illusion.

"The staff has been working all day, Susan," Charles said coolly. "What do you think of the preparations?"

"They're splendid, Charles," she said, slamming back down to earth with a jolt. She usually spent time helping decorate. Today she'd been too concerned about looking appealing tonight—for Thatch.

She saw that Charles was dressed as a conquistador. Appropriate, she thought—or was it symbolic? She didn't have time to ponder the question as the passengers began to fill the room with their excited chatter and varied outfits, from Mexican costumes to American designer clothing.

Almost every ensemble was topped by gorgeous jewels. This was the shining night, the occasion for bringing out the most lavish jewelry. Ladies and gentlemen alike sparkled and glittered, as Charles had so tactlessly said, with so much razzle-dazzle that some of them were lit up!

The mariachis, in their *charro*-style regalia and huge sombreros, began strumming their guitars, strolling among the crowd, singing Christmas carols in Spanish, favorites that were clearly recognizable to almost anyone in any language.

The high-spirited crowd of party-goers swarmed around the buffet tables, sampling food, laughing loudly, savoring the catered holiday on the high seas.

Susan and Thatch relished the party, too. When the American band began to play dance music, the pretty Mexican dancer and the handsome bearded matador were one of the first couples on the floor. They couldn't wait a moment longer to hold each other. Susan slipped into Thatch's embrace as if she'd been created for his arms alone. Thatch held her to his heart, as if he never intended to let her go.

The music changed in tempo; the songs came and went, and Thatch and Susan were separated more than once by an over-eager or rowdy intruder who wanted a new dance partner, but those moments didn't exist for them. The only time that mattered was when they were together.

Even though Thatch was vaguely alerted to the dissension created by Merry Lou when Eva turned up with Sir Roger Nester, he had no intention of facing anything unpleasant tonight unless he was literally forced. He was also aware that Merry Lou was making a fuss, insisting on dancing with Charles, but he didn't notice that, when she did dance with him, she repeatedly pointed to both Eva and Roger and Susan and himself.

Thatch and Susan danced on, neither of them sampling anything sweeter than the sight of each other. Thatch almost couldn't believe it when he heard the familiar *Auld Lang Syne*, in both English and Spanish. He'd always associated the song with New Year's Eve, yet it seemed so right this Christmas Eve, with Susan in his arms.

At the stroke of midnight, people began to exchange gifts, their talk and laughter growing louder and louder, the merriment at its peak, the band playing boisterously, a Mexican Santa Claus putting in an appearance for revelers young and old.

"Let's ride that horse to the sunset now," Thatch whispered for Susan's ears alone. "I want you all to myself. I have something special for you."

Susan had something special for Thatch, too. She was more than ready to ride off into the sunset, or rather, the black night. She wanted to escape the lively party-goers and spend time alone with Thatch.

In moments, he had whisked her through the crowd, his hand at her elbow, oblivious to everyone around them. They took the elevator to the Fiesta Deck, where, to Thatch's surprise, the music filtered up, but the clatter and chatter of the party people didn't.

Taking her in his arms again, out on the isolated dimly lit deck, he kissed her gently, his lips clinging warmly and softly to hers.

"I've been wanting to do that all night," he said thickly.

Susan wrapped her arms around his neck and pressed her body close to his. "Don't let me go, Thatch," she whispered. "I want this night to last forever."

He held her close to his heart again and began to turn her to the strains of the music drifting up to the top deck. He forgot all about the gift he had for her. He, too, wanted this night to last forever.

Sighing in contentment, he slid his hands over her back and waist, loving the feel of her, treasuring the warmth of her in his embrace.

Susan rested her head on Thatch's shoulder as they traveled somewhere she'd never been before on the ship, even though they only moved around and around in small circles. She could feel the muscled contours of Thatch's body as he held her, his thigh between hers as he danced with her, skillfully and flawlessly matching his movements to her own, never once stumbling or faltering.

Dawn was pushing at the edges of night when the couple finally stopped dancing. They didn't know when the party had ended, or when the band had left. They had listened to the music in their hearts and the band had played on. Neither of them recalled that they had Christmas presents to exchange. Their gifts were each other and this rare and precious time.

Only the steady slapping of sports shoes against the deck as a jogger took an early-morning run roused the couple from the magical web they had spun around themselves, secreting each other away from the rest of the ship.

"Merry Christmas," the jogger called out cheerily, eliciting a reluctant response from Thatch and Susan.

When they had returned the greeting and the jogger had sped on, Thatch murmured, "Merry Christmas, Susan."

"Merry Christmas, Thatch," she whispered, her voice husky.

"I'll see you to your room," he said thickly, drawing Susan against his side, unwilling to relinquish her just yet.

She looked slightly dazed by the breaking of morning. "It is late," she murmured.

"Or early," he said, placing a kiss on her forehead. "It was a wonderful party, Susan. The most wonderful I think I've ever attended."

"Mmm," she said wistfully, "me, too. I wish it didn't have to end."

He chuckled. "I think it ended hours ago, sweetheart."

"Oh," she said, the single word a sigh of disappointment.

"There will be other parties, won't there?" he asked, looking into her brown eyes.

Susan wasn't sure what he was asking. Yes, there were other parties scheduled on the ship.

But would there be other parties, magic parties for her and Thatch?

Chapter Nine

Thatch didn't get to sleep until it was almost time for breakfast. He'd heard the dining room was having open seating all day. Many people were going ashore for the entire week in Acapulco, having already arranged hotel accommodations as part of the package.

Thatch had done that, too, to be where the passengers were staying, although he knew some were only spending a night or two, then returning to the ship. He'd booked the entire week, even though he planned to go back and forth, depending on the action or lack of it.

He had expected Susan to stay on the ship, as almost every member of the crew did, in part because it was economical, and also because some of the passengers stayed and the staff had to work. There was another party planned tonight, on a smaller scale than last night's. Thatch was waiting for the right moment to give his present to Susan. Eva's would keep, but after last night, he wanted to use the necklace he'd gotten Susan to open up some necessary conversation.

He knew that he was getting more deeply involved with her by the day, and though he wanted to trust fate, his training and ingrained suspicions forbade him to abandon himself any more recklessly than he already had. There were things he needed to talk to her about, not necessarily having to do with her past, yet definitely having to do with her future—*their* future.

Susan slept a total of two hours, then struggled forth to do her aquatic-exercise class. She was afraid she would fall asleep during it, but fortunately Charles put the music on louder than usual, and there were only a handful of participants, some who'd partied too hearty and come to the workout because of guilt, and some diehards who never missed.

When the session was over, Susan dried herself with a thick towel, slipped her feet into flip-flops and started back to her room. Charles caught her arm before she could get very far.

"I need to talk to you," he said.

"Oh, not now, please, Charles," she murmured. "I'm exhausted. Can't it wait until I get a cup of coffee and a roll?"

"It's about your friend Thatch," he said, eyes gleaming.

At the mention of the name, Susan's heart picked up its pace, and suddenly she was no longer sleepy. "What about him?"

"Oh, you *can* manage a few minutes for me when it concerns him, can you?" Charles asked sourly.

Sighing, Susan said, "Charles, please don't talk to me just to be hateful. If you have something to say, say it. If you don't, let me pull myself together."

Charles freed her arm. "By all means, Susan, go pull yourself together. I think you'll need all your wits about you when you hear what I have to say."

"What are you talking about?" she asked, her heart beating alarmingly.

He shrugged. "You need time to pull yourself together, remember? This will wait. I still have to get some further information—incriminating information, if I'm correct—anyway."

"Oh, Charles!" she cried in frustration. "Not that silliness again. No one's been burglarized. You're acting maliciously, and I won't indulge it."

Charles caught her arm again and drew her near, causing her damp braid to slap wetly against her back. "No one's been burglarized yet, but I have it on good authority that your 'Thatch' uses that name as a foil. Someone aboard ship is reasonably sure his real name is Thaddeus Waller."

Susan's instinctive desire to defend Thatch almost had her saying that Thatch was no doubt a nickname for Thaddeus, but she knew as well as Charles that there was no explaining the fact that Thatch had said his name was Daniel Thatcher.

"Let go of me," she said instead, not knowing what else to say. Her pulse was racing. Surely there was some explanation. The "someone" had to be wrong!

"Maybe I *am* being silly!" Charles said suddenly, as if he'd been struck by an idea. "Why should anyone face the man down *before* he does something? I don't know what I'm thinking of! We all want the burglar caught. There's plenty of time to confront your *Mr. Thatcher,* isn't there? Why, the trip is only half-over, and you're right, nothing's been stolen. Yet.''

"And nothing will be—at least, not by Thatch," Susan shot back, "because he is not the burglar. You talk about not wanting more bad press, Charles. Well, harassing an innocent man is just that."

"Is it, my dear?" he said, pretending to be pensive. "Indeed, I suppose I have no reason to direct any notice to him at this point. That will only scare him away, won't it? But I warn you, Susan, use your brain. Have enough sense to be suspicious of the man. And don't warn him off now that I've alerted you."

"I told you before, Charles," she said testily, "you're behaving badly because you're jealous. Thatch isn't the man you want to make him out to be. He doesn't even care about money."

"Oh?" Charles said. "Did he tell you that, or were you foolish enough to tell him how rich you are? Have you gone and done that yet, Susan Williams? Just how much does the man know about you? And how much do you know about him? Floating about the dance floor in his arms doesn't qualify you as an expert, in case you don't know."

"Can't you hear how petty you sound, Charles?" she asked, although tension was building in her stomach. She hadn't told Thatch much about herself. It shouldn't matter to him that she was rich, if he loved her. What counted was love. She would never do what her mother did—marry a man for money. She'd heard all her life how pretty Julia Harriston "caught" Jonathan Stonehall Williams.

Susan sucked in her breath. *If he loved her,* she repeated to herself. No one had said anything about love. She was jumping to conclusions faster than Charles was. In fact, she recalled all too clearly, she'd been the one to pursue Thatch, not the other way around.

"Doesn't it occur to you that Thatcher's one proficient con man to have won you over so quickly, Susan?" Charles continued. "No one has ever done that before. Believe me," he said bitterly, "I know. The man probably knows all about you. Maybe he's discovered theft is kid stuff when he can woo money!"

"Stop it, Charles!" Susan cried. "He doesn't know I'm rich! You and management are the only ones on the ship who know that, so stop speculating!"

Her outburst seemed to take the wind out of his sails, but only momentarily. He looked a little perplexed, then began again.

"And why haven't you told him, Susan? Don't you trust him? Well, believe me, my dear, you shouldn't! He was using the alias Thaddeus Waller when he proposed to Merry Lou Addison. She's the someone who told me, correctly pointing out Mr. Thatcher as the imposter while we danced last night. I gather he must have thought she was wealthy, but she ended the relationship before any real damage was done."

Susan was taken aback! Could this be true? Stunned by the mere possibility, she dashed down the deck as if the devil himself were after her.

Charles had succeeded at least partly in doing what he'd come to do. He'd caused fresh doubts to rise in Susan's mind: doubts about herself and Thatch. Thatch had promised her nothing. Nothing at all. And he'd told her almost nothing. He had been elusive and evasive all right; still, she couldn't believe he had anything to do with the thefts. She didn't want to believe he'd had anything to do with Merry Lou Addison!

Without consciously thinking about what she was doing, Susan rushed to the Júbilo Deck. She was breathless and still damp by the time she reached Thatch's door and rapped on it.

Startled from a deep sleep, Thatch struggled to wake up enough to be fully alert to handle he knew not what. He pulled on a pair of shorts over the briefs he'd slept in and struggled to make some sense of the time. It was still early morning. He'd danced all night. Literally! He was bone weary and exuberant at the same time.

Running both hands through his hair, he blinked his eyes open wide a couple of times, then opened the door. "Susan!" he cried, surprised to see her, and instantly realizing that she was distressed. "What's wrong?"

She licked her lips and wondered why on earth she'd rushed down here like a dummy. Poor Thatch had been sound asleep. She shivered, only now realizing that she still had on her wet bathing suit.

"May I come in, Thatch?" she whispered, needing him very much at the moment. She didn't know what she would say or what he would say, but she needed to hear the right responses from Thatch.

"Yes, of course," he said, opening the door wider. He pulled her into his arms, holding her damp body against his warm one, feeling her trembling. "What's wrong, sweetheart?" he asked. "Tell me."

Susan clung to him, feeling his naked chest against her wet breasts, feeling his hips against hers, his thighs muscled and warm. Laying her head on his shoulder, she whispered, "Thatch, do you think I'm rich?"

She could feel him tense the moment the words left her mouth. Immediately he felt as chilled as she. She didn't understand why, but it frightened her down to the very pit of her soul. Did he know she was rich and think she didn't know he knew? Or did he not know she was rich and would not take kindly to the idea if she was? Or worse—had Charles been right?

She couldn't bear to think about the last possibility. It seemed that many moments passed before Thatch said anything, moments in which Susan went a little crazy.

Thatch didn't know what had prompted the question, and he was totally unprepared for it. Why had Susan come to him now to ask him? The adrenaline was racing through his body, for he sensed his answer was crucial. But why? To Susan? To the case he was working on? Or just because she had decided to let him know more about her?

The last thought struck him as erroneous, leaving him in more of a quandary. He didn't think he could evade the truth anymore, but he didn't quite see how he could tell her, either. Even though it seemed simple enough to say something such as he'd heard she had money, self-preservation warned him against that. If only he knew what had precipitated the question.

Becoming more and more afraid, Susan looked into his eyes. "Thatch?" she murmured.

He held her tightly against him, trying to stop her trembling but it didn't help. She wanted an answer to her question.

"Susan, sweetheart," he said, meeting her eyes, "what's this all about? What are you talking about? Why would I think a working woman like you is rich?"

"Do you, Thatch?" she asked, hurt and determination in her voice.

Thatch felt as if all his skills were about to fail him. What he said to her now mattered very much for their future. He lifted her chin with one hand while he kept the other wrapped around her tightly.

"No," he said, "I don't think you're rich. What's this all about?"

Hope flared in those fearful brown eyes. Thatch felt his heart sinking. He kept telling himself that he didn't *know* she was rich. For all he knew, the information he'd gathered had changed now. Hadn't he himself thought that perhaps the family business was in trouble and that was one possibility for the thefts?

Of course, that was when he'd considered Susan a suspect. He knew this woman was no thief. Why had she come to him with this question?

"Is that the truth, Thatch?" she asked so somberly, so sincerely, that he felt like telling her what he was doing on the ship and what he'd read about her.

Yet, he couldn't do that. Not because he didn't trust her, but because he had ethics, and they wouldn't allow him to divulge any information on the case that could inadvertently jeopardize it. Something or someone had set her off, had sent her running to his room, and he would have to play out his hand until he knew why.

He was hoping and praying it was because she was falling for him just as he was falling for her, and she wanted him to know who she was.

He was disappointed.

Susan searched his face for a moment, then backed out of his arms. She looked confused and uncertain, yet relieved, too.

"I feel so foolish," she murmured, brushing at her bangs and the damp tendrils that had escaped her braid when she'd laid her head on his shoulder. She looked around distractedly, and Thatch knew that she was going to lie to him about why she was here.

Her eyes met his again. "Many kinds of people travel on ships, Thatch. Some good, some not so good, some indifferent, some downright no good. A few men—and women—come aboard ship looking for vulnerable, lonely people they can take advantage of. Some of them do it only to get to those people's money."

The last thing in the world Thatch wanted to do at this moment was make light of the situation, but it seemed the only way out for both of them.

"Is that what you think I've done, Susan?" he asked, forcing a grin. "Do you think I'm on board to take advantage of you, to take your money? How much money do you make a trip, anyway?" He pretended to count on his fingers. "Let's see, with tips—you do get tips, don't you?" he asked, looking at her.

Susan felt like an utter fool. She began to laugh. "Oh, Thatch, I'm sorry. I must sound like an absolute idiot to you. It's just that—that—" *that I'm in-*

credibly, embarrassingly, filthy rich, she wanted to say and couldn't. "It's just that someone told me you thought I had money."

He forced himself to laugh. "Was he a friend or enemy?"

Susan pondered the question for a moment. "I don't know," she answered honestly.

Thatch was still holding her chin between his thumb and forefinger. He lowered his head and caressed her trembling mouth with his firm lips. He wanted to ease her discomfort, to see the dimpled, extroverted woman he knew was beneath this frightened one, but he didn't possess the power to make that happen at the moment. He touched her mouth with his a second time, then he freed her.

Susan was still standing there, her lips parted, her eyes closed. She wanted more of his touch, more of his reassurance.

"You'd better go have a hot shower before you catch pneumonia," he said gently. "Or before I really take advantage of you. You look much too tempting standing here in my room in that swimsuit."

He bent down and picked up the towel that had fallen away from her neck. "You must have taught your exercise class."

She nodded, slowly coming out of her drugged state as Thatch placed the towel around her shoulders again. Briefly she thought how nice it would be for Thatch to continue. She imagined him kissing her thoroughly, his warm hands on her skin, his—

"Yes," she said, before she could get too carried away in her mind. She snuggled into the towel. "Suddenly I'm very, very sleepy. I think I'll go back to bed.''

Inadvertently she glanced at Thatch's rumpled bed, thinking that sleep wasn't exactly what was on her mind at the moment.

Thatch felt a quickening inside him. He would like nothing better than to take Susan to that very bed this moment and make sweet, sweet love to her. But that wasn't wise, either.

Needing desperately to keep his hands busy, he unconsciously stroked his beard. He was startled to feel the unfamiliar hair. He was also reminded that he was on this ship to do a job.

As if Susan had known what a dangerous turn Thatch's thoughts had taken when his gaze raked over the bed, her face turned bright red. She slid her fingers along her neck repeatedly.

Recognizing the nervous gesture, Thatch stilled her fingers with his own.

''I woke you up,'' she said foolishly, still looking at the rumpled bed.

''That's okay,'' he murmured, intertwining her fingers in his. ''I'll fall back to sleep in minutes. Then I'll wake up starving. Will you meet me in the dining room at eleven?''

She nodded.

''All right. Get warm and get some rest,'' Thatch said, practically pulling her toward the door. Then he shut it before he could draw her back into his arms.

Facing the bed again, he knew that there would be a day of reckoning between him and Susan. It was inevitable. He also knew in his heart that it was going to hurt like hell.

Susan stood outside Thatch's room for a moment. She'd only asked one question. In her eagerness to believe that he truly didn't know she was rich, she'd forgotten to ask the other one.

Was Thatch also known as Thaddeus Waller? Had Merry Lou Addison told Charles the truth?

Thatch found the ship still in full swing for the Christmas holiday when he went to lunch. He'd pulled on the first pair of slacks and shirt he'd found, then discovered that the others were dressed in their finery for the occasion.

"Over here, Thatch," Mrs. Nossam called, indicating their table.

Thatch waved a hand in acknowledgment. When he saw Susan talking animatedly with Charles, who was glowering at her disapprovingly, Thatch exhaled heavily. He'd barely begun to believe in human goodness again. He didn't want to confront Charles's jealousy today. He made his way to the table, where his regular companions were.

"For you," Mrs. Nossam said, handing him a package.

Thatch felt a rush of guilt. Even though he had Susan's necklace in his shirt pocket, it had never occurred to him to get anything for the Nossams, or the others at his table. His face reddened as one after another, they shared in the spirit of giving by handing him wrapped gifts.

"You really shouldn't have," he muttered, hating the old cliché, and feeling guilty. He'd been selfish, he thought, in not thinking of them when they'd all remembered him. He was flattered.

Lois Threadlam gazed fondly at Harry. "We all bought something for each other, and we didn't want you to be left out."

Thatch wished he had something—*anything*—to give them, but then the point wasn't to give them something merely because they were giving him something. They had acted from the heart, not from guilt. The least he could do was be gracious.

"Open them!" Sheila Azor urged.

Thatch could feel his face burn as he looked for Susan. For some silly reason, he wanted her to see that the others had given him gifts. He was astonished at how sentimental he was feeling.

He hadn't realized how vulnerable and suspicious he'd become after working as a private investigator for so long. He'd decided that almost everyone had an ulterior motive for being nice, yet clearly these people only wanted to make his holiday more pleasant.

He smiled in relief when he saw Susan heading in his direction. She had a small bag in her hand.

"Hello," she said brightly to the others.

"I think you all know Susan," Thatch said, realizing how proud he was of her. He was enlightened to realize that he was proud of his tablemates, too. They had many better qualities than he'd given them credit for the first day, and not just because they'd shared gifts with him. As they greeted Susan, he thought about what likable people they were, despite their little idiosyncrasies.

"It's refreshing to be able to share some individual time with you all," Susan said as Thatch gave her his chair and dragged another one from an empty table.

"Look what they gave me," Thatch told her, his face still flushed.

Susan laughed. He was wearing his bashful-boy look, and she loved it. "And here are your gifts for them," she said, handing him the bag.

He quickly covered his puzzlement when he realized that Susan was rescuing him. "Thanks for bringing them," he said, feeling more grateful than deceitful.

"Well, I couldn't let you hand them out unwrapped as you wanted to do," she said, rolling her eyes as she looked at the other women. "Men!" she said in pretended exasperation.

Thatch started taking the gifts from the bag, more than thankful that Susan had wrapped the majority of them in red—for the ladies he was sure, and the other two in green, for the gents.

"Thanks," he said. "But they're just going to rip up the paper, anyway."

"That's part of the fun," she insisted, brown eyes glowing, as she discreetly handed out the presents herself. They were all wrapped alike, although they were a little different in shape. Thatch wondered how Susan could possibly determine who would get what and why it would matter.

Thatch thought of the necklace he had in his pocket for Susan. While it wasn't wrapped, at least it was in a box.

"You still haven't opened your presents, Thatch," Mrs. Nossam said. "We're all waiting."

He smiled, then set about ripping off the paper. He was surprised by the thoughtful collection of Mexican business supplies he received from the group: a paperweight in the shape of a sombrero, a pen shaped like a bottle of tequila, and beautifully detailed bull-fighter bookends.

"You might be the only man in insurance in L.A. with that particular decor in your office," Mrs. Nossam said happily.

A new rush of guilt ran over Thatch. Damn it, he was just doing his job, but he'd never felt so bad about misrepresenting himself to people.

"I think you're right, and I'm delighted," he managed to say. "Now please open your presents."

"We really didn't expect these," Lois said, gently removing the paper from hers.

Neither did I, Thatch thought, wondering what Susan had gotten and why. The gifts were apparently little trinkets she kept on hand for emergencies. Regardless, Thatch was grateful, and he meant to repay her for saving the day.

"Oh, how lovely!" Lois cried, removing a delicate necklace from a box. "You really shouldn't have! Oh, Thatch, this is much too expensive. I can't take it."

"Of course you can," Susan insisted, smiling at the other woman. "It will look beautiful on you."

Thatch swallowed. Who had Susan gotten the necklace for? It had cost a pretty penny, he was sure, and he wasn't even a connoisseur of jewelry. He thought again how rich Susan must be, and wondered why she'd come to his room so agitated this morning. They really had to talk. And soon.

"Look at mine!" Mrs. Nossam exclaimed, as excited as if she'd discovered a pirate's treasure at the bottom of the ocean. Although she was bedecked in diamonds today, she was clearly genuinely thrilled to think Thatch had purchased the gold chain with the matador on it just for her.

He was rather stunned himself, even though he should have expected it after Lois's necklace. Neither piece was costume jewelry. He was just recovering from Mrs. Nossam's gift when Sheila suddenly reached over and bussed him on the cheek.

"Bless you!" she exclaimed. "Why, no man has remembered me in such a special way since Cloy died."

Thatch was hesitant to even glance at the gift she'd received. There were tears in her eyes, and he was touched.

There was no avoiding the present. Sheila held the delicate necklace up for all to see. "It's a miniature bouquet of flowers," she said, her voice husky.

Thatch believed Susan had shown amazing perception with this group. He was impressed, and grew even more so when the men opened their presents to find gold cuff links.

Even Mr. Nossam, who didn't seem to have much to say unless his wife prompted him, was enthusiastic. "How nice to have a man select my cuff links," he said. "They've got some gusto!" Thatch grinned. Gusto, indeed. They were *charros*—Mexican cowboys. Harry's were pretty Mexican girls.

"Yours might have gusto," he joked, "but mine have lust-o!"

He winked at Lois, then held his hand out to Thatch.

Hell! Thatch felt like a fraud again. He'd have felt much better if Susan had given *little* remembrances. He couldn't imagine whom she'd actually purchased

the gifts for. Someone was going to be terribly disappointed at not receiving them.

"Are you two having lunch with us?" Mrs. Nossam asked, after the gift-giving was over.

"Actually we're going to take plates up to the Fiesta Deck," Susan said, wanting to be alone with
Thatch, knowing she had to talk to him.

"Yes," he added, "we'd already made those plans."
Another lie, even if it was told in good cause. Then
that's what he said about them all.

The men offered Susan the courtly gesture of
standing when she rose. Thatch was even more impressed with his newfound friends. He was really feeling good about life and people in general when he put
his gifts into the bag Susan had carried the others in,
slid the handles over his arm and guided Susan toward the buffet tables.

People everywhere were calling out Merry Christmas, and Thatch heard himself responding in kind. It
was hard to believe that only last year he'd been the
bah-humbug type.

He was feeling so optimistic about life and himself
that he was totally unprepared for Susan's question
when they entered the elevator to ride to the top deck,
plates of food in one hand, beverages juggled in the
other.

"Who is Thaddeus Waller?"

Thatch fought mightily against turning red. He
usually managed to field these on-the-spot questions
amazingly well. But not with this woman. Not with
Susan Williams, who'd gotten to him too much for
him to blatantly lie yet again to her.

"Why do you ask?" he said. "Am I supposed to know him?"

Susan was determined not to be put off. "Merry Lou Addison claims you do."

Hell! Merry Lou Addison did indeed seem to be tracking him! Why? Because of her interest in Roger and anger at Eva? Surely she couldn't know that Eva and Thatch were cohorts, could she? Had she discovered he'd lied about not being Thaddeus?

"What made her say that?" he asked, still trying to ward off the inevitable.

Susan held his gaze, and he wondered if those big brown eyes could see right through him. The car came to a stop, the doors opened, and still Susan stared at him.

"She told Charles she knows you from the past and that you said you were Thaddeus Waller. She says you tried to marry her."

Oh, Lord! Thatch thought, his mind whirling.

"Charles thinks you're the jewelry thief," Susan continued in that steadfast way of hers, not waiting for an explanation to her first revelation.

Thatch wanted to laugh. This was a fine kettle of fish. He thought Charles was possibly the thief. The only puzzle was why he would steal from a ship he'd invested in. A small sum, it was true, but he'd invested all the same. It didn't make sense for him to commit the thefts, thereby further damaging the ship's reputation and his investment.

"And what do you think?" Thatch asked, trying to motivate Susan to leave the elevator. He was getting claustrophobic.

"I don't know what to think," she said, holding her ground.

Fortunately several other Christmas revelers came into the car, wishing the couple a Merry Christmas and asking if they were going down.

Thatch and Susan returned the greeting, albeit halfheartedly, then left.

"Is that why you asked if I thought you were rich?" Thatch said, his training coming to the forefront as he tried to avoid an out-and-out confrontation, which could only harm them at this point.

"Do you?" she repeated.

Thatch stared at her for a moment, then went over to a lounge chair and perched on the edge, setting the plate of food and the beverage on the deck between his feet. The bag of presents fell off his arm and hit the floor. He was no longer concerned with them.

"Listen, Susan," he said in a low, tight voice, "there are a lot of things you don't understand here, and I'm simply not at liberty to tell you."

She was standing in front of him, her plate and drink still in hand. Thatch saw her fingers begin to tremble. Turning on her heel, she tossed the food in the nearest trash container and strode off.

"Susan, stop!" Thatch called, racing to catch up with her, knocking his drink over in the process.

"Get away from me, Thatch—or whoever you are!" she demanded.

He grasped her shoulders and made her look at him. "I'd like to do just that, Susan Williams, but I'm in love with you. I can't just go away."

When he saw her brown eyes widen, he pressed what he hoped was an advantage. "Just give me a little time and a whole lot of trust and this will work out, I promise you."

It had to, he told himself. He hadn't acknowledged to himself how much he loved this woman until she'd walked away.

"I don't believe you for a moment," she said, though he could see the hesitancy and the hope in her expression. Her full, pink mouth trembled, and her dark eyes were full of fear and questions.

"Susan," he said softly, "I told you earlier that situations and people aren't always as they seem. You haven't been honest with me, either, and you and I both know it. You didn't purchase those presents you passed out to the passengers at my table from some five-and-dime store."

"I know the Christmas ritual on these cruises," she said defensively. "Everyone feels generous. I was afraid it wouldn't occur to you to get gifts for them. They've traveled before, and they know it's customary to give everyone at the table a little something. I keep little trinkets on hand for such occasions, or when someone doesn't get anything at all."

"The gold necklaces and cuff links weren't little trinkets," he said. Before she had time to respond, he added, "I'm sure you have your reasons for keeping your past private, just as I have. We both know they have to be aired, but not now. If you care for me at all, give me a little time."

So he did know she was rich! Charles was right! Susan had known all along a shipboard romance was never going to work. Still, oh, how it hurt to think Thatch was an imposter, that he might have proposed to Merry Lou for her money, that he was after *her* money! She should have had better sense than to give such expensive gifts.

It occurred to her that perhaps she'd purchased them unconsciously because she wanted Thatch to know the truth about her and didn't know how to tell him. While it was a fact that she did keep a supply of trinkets, they weren't the expensive items she'd purchased just for his table.

She didn't know what to do. Thatch had said he loved her. Was it possible? He'd also already admitted they didn't even know each other.

What was he hiding? And how much did it matter? No, she didn't believe that Thatch was a thief, but who was the real Thatch? What was he?

Unexpectedly he reached into his shirt pocket and pulled out his gift for her. "Take this and wear it near your heart until we can work this out, Susan," he murmured, opening the box so that she could see the necklace was a diamond pendant.

Susan stared at it a moment, then shook her head and turned away. She didn't know what to think. She did know she didn't want Thatch or anything connected to him any closer to her heart than he already was!

"No, thanks, Thatch. You keep it. And this, too!"

She tossed a tiny package onto the nearest lounge chair and left before he could see the tears swimming in her sad eyes.

Chapter Ten

Intuition told Thatch there was no point in pursuing Susan now. She needed time to herself to digest what he'd said. He stared after her, wanting more than anything in the world to take her in his arms and tell her everything.

But he couldn't. He looked at the necklace he'd purchased for her, wishing he'd gotten a diamond engagement ring and she had accepted it, though of course it was much too soon for such things.

He sighed tiredly. He never gave up until he got his man—or his woman. In this case, Susan Williams—the woman he wanted for a lifetime. He wasn't about to give up. His timing was simply off.

Picking up the package, he quickly opened it. To his surprise, he found a man's diamond solitaire ring. He stared at it for a moment, his mind spinning. He took the ring out of the box and slipped it on the third finger of his left hand. He smiled at the perfect fit.

Then he tossed his food into the trash receptacle and returned to his room. When he dialed Susan's room, he could tell by her voice that she'd been weeping.

"Susan," he said gently, "don't—"

She hung up before he could finish. He dialed again. The phone rang and rang. He hung up, paced his room a few minutes, then dialed again.

She answered this time, probably thinking he'd given up. "Don't hang up, please," he pleaded. "Just listen for a minute."

He could hear her breathing raggedly. She didn't speak, but she didn't hang up, either. "I accept," he said. He waited a moment, knowing she had to be curious about what he was accepting. Then he added, "I accept your ring, and I consider us properly engaged."

He could hear her intake of breath, then she replaced the phone. Thatch smiled again. He believed he knew Susan well enough to know that she would think about what he'd said. She might still be angry and uncertain and believe he had incredible gall to say such a thing. But she hadn't slammed the phone down.

Susan would be on the ship the same length of time as Thatch. He would wait, and he hoped she would give him the time he needed to set things straight. Now it was past time to get on with the job he'd come here to do.

Merry Lou Addison was moved right to the top of his suspect list; she bore some checking into. Maybe she was merely a woman set on revenge because he knew her past, or maybe his appearance on the ship interfered with her pursuit of money, in this particular case, jewels. He was determined to find out.

Susan stared at the phone. Thatch was crazy! He was perverse! Charles was right. He was shady!

She sat down on the edge of her bed and exhaled. Thatch wasn't any of those things and she knew it. She didn't exactly know what he was, yet she believed in her heart that he really did have an explanation for whatever was going on. She just didn't know what. Or what it would mean to her.

He'd said he loved her. She couldn't forget that. She wanted to believe it, because she was sure if he really did love her, everything was going to be okay.

She frowned. She didn't know why, but she did believe it! Lifting her chin high, she tried to cheer up. There was nothing to do except get on with her responsibilities.

Bravely, she got ready to go out among the passengers who'd chosen not to go ashore at Acapulco. Christmas Day was being celebrated on the ship. She had another party to attend.

The only betraying sign of her inner fear and turmoil was the single stubborn tear that insisted on slipping down her cheek. She brushed at it with her fist, as a small child might. Then she got on with business.

At the hotel where almost all the passengers who went ashore were staying, Thatch had a seemingly innocuous rendezvous with Eva when he encountered her sitting alone in the hotel restaurant overlooking a lovely beach.

"Eva Adkins, isn't it?" he asked, pausing by her table.

She extended her hand. "Yes, Mr. Thatcher. The man who rescued my pearls."

They shook hands. "Merry Lou Addison's a repeat passenger with a passion for pearls and a past history of getting them any way she can," he murmured quietly. "She was on the last three cruises."

Eva nodded, rummaged around in her roomy purse and handed him a present. "Merry Christmas," she said, smiling happily. "This is in gratitude for your retrieving my pearls."

She indicated a chair. "Won't you sit down?"

Thatch nodded. "Thank you. I can only stay a moment. I have something for you, too." He took a small gift from his shirt pocket and handed it to her.

"Let's open them now," she urged, still smiling brightly.

Thatch opened his to find a slim date book for the new year. He flipped through it, barely glancing at the notes Eva had made for him concerning passengers on the suspect list.

"Thank you for the personal inscription," he said. "I'm sure I'll get a lot of use out of this."

She opened her gift, a compact calendar for the new year with brief notes Thatch had made, particularly on Merry Lou.

"A very merry Christmas," he said, standing up.

"I think so," she said, her smile still intact. "Enjoy Acapulco."

"You, too."

* * *

The week in Acapulco sped by with amazing swiftness. Thatch and Eva were sure the thief would strike while the passengers were off the ship. They alternated, each one furtively spying on Merry Lou and other suspects who stayed on the ship throughout the Acapulco layover, but no thefts occurred.

They were disappointed, for they had settled on Merry Lou Addison as the supreme suspect. She had motive—lack of money after she'd been divorced by her wealthy husband. She also had the opportunity— she'd aggressively made friends with other older wealthy women, going in and out of their cabins frequently. She also had a history of lack of integrity.

Thatch and Eva played the waiting game to no avail. They began to wonder if they should reconsider their list. Charles hadn't been completely ruled out, although chances seemed slim that he was the thief.

Sir Roger Nester was still on Thatch's list, but it seemed that Eva had succumbed to his charms as badly as Thatch had succumbed to Susan's. Eva didn't believe he was guilty, despite his pretending to be wealthy when information proved he wasn't.

Thatch had to give Eva the same talk she'd given him about not losing her perspective in such glamorous surroundings with a charming man. And even though Eva stuck to her belief that the burglar wasn't Roger, she insisted she would, and could, be objective.

Mexico Magic sailed from Acapulco with Thatch and Eva no further along in solving the thefts than they'd been when the ship dropped anchor. Thatch had managed to see a little of the exciting city of Acapulco and change Susan's Christmas present. Other than that, the time was wasted.

Thatch had kept his distance from Susan when he was on and off the ship, trying to be totally absorbed in his work, but back on the open ocean he found it impossible to stay away from the woman he loved.

The first day at sea, he turned up for aquatic-exercise classes, the diamond Susan had given him worn prominently on his finger where it had been since he'd opened her gift.

Susan couldn't believe her eyes when he slipped into the pool and began the workout. She had never felt more awkward in her life. Somehow she got through the session, but all she wanted to do was hurry away when it was over. Grabbing a towel, she didn't even bother to dry herself as she poked her feet into her flip-flops and began to walk away.

Today, New Year's Eve, was the second busiest day of the three-week trip, and she had a thousand things on her mind. She didn't need to add Thatch to the list. She'd managed to stay reasonably sane during the Acapulco layover by keeping occupied, though he'd helped by staying away.

"Susan!"

She spun around at the sound of her name. Charles turned, too.

"What does he want now?" he bit out. "I thought you'd wised up and were avoiding him."

Susan didn't comment. She couldn't, and even if she could have, she knew that the only reason she'd been able to keep her distance from Thatch was that he'd worked it that way. Her heart pounding, she stood stiffly, wondering herself what he would say.

To her surprise, he inquired casually, "Can I rent a tux here on the ship? I didn't bring anything for the New Year's Eve party."

She couldn't believe how incredibly disappointed she was. She had expected anything except that question. Anything!

"Yes," she mumbled. "Check with the Esquire on the Sea shop."

"Thanks," he said, smiling brightly. He nodded at the scowling Charles. "Good day." And then he was gone.

Susan stared after him. Did he know the turmoil he caused her? Did he care?

"Come, Susan," Charles said, speaking sharply for the first time in days, "we have to check on the New Year's Eve party arrangements."

She nodded blindly. She didn't care about the party. She cared about Thatch, and the price for caring was getting higher all the time.

That evening, Thatch gazed at his image in the mirror. "Hell, Thatch," he muttered aloud, "you've never looked so good. Then you've never worn a tux, and you've never planned such an evening."

He smoothed his hair, grinned proudly at himself and sauntered out of his cabin. It was New Year's Eve, and he intended to make the coming year the best of his life.

Susan felt her heart flutter madly when she finally spied Thatch walking into the ballroom. She was sure he'd purposely arrived late, adding to her anxiety. She'd dressed with special care, but she felt like Cinderella before the night of the ball when she saw Thatch. Goodness, he was handsome! The handsome prince. And her without a glass slipper.

To her surprise, he walked directly to her, ignoring all others in his path, keeping his eyes on her alone. She couldn't look away from him. She tried and found it impossible.

"You are the most beautiful woman here," he said when he reached her. "I'm proud you're going to be my wife."

"Thatch," she murmured frantically, glancing at the people around her who could hear him perfectly, "what are you saying?"

He held up his left hand. "Our engagement," he said casually. He took her ring from his pocket. "Here, try this."

"Thatch . . ." she growled, but he ignored her and lifted her left hand.

"Ah, my guess wasn't quite as accurate as yours," he murmured disappointedly, seeing that the ring was a little big. "Never mind," he said. "We'll have it altered when we get to L.A."

He slid it from her finger and Susan was too shocked to do anything except stare from Thatch to the people around her, who were already buzzing excitedly with the news.

"Thatch . . ." she began again.

He smiled. "You keep saying that. I already told you I accept. We're engaged." He then slid the diamond ring on her middle finger. "This will have to do for now," he said.

Susan grasped his hands, pulling him away from the others. "Thatch!"

"You're hung up on that name," he murmured, going with her. The music had started, and he drew her into his arms.

"What else am I supposed to call you?" she asked as they danced. "Thaddeus Waller?"

"What an ugly name!" he said playfully. "No, Thatch will do. But let's keep it a secret between us for now. It's all right for an engaged couple to have secrets, don't you think?"

"We're not engaged. We don't even know each other."

"I'm doing my best to rectify that," he said, "and I want the same openness and trust from you." His voice was earnest suddenly. "It's not easy, Susan. I've been growing progressively more cynical over the years—until you. You entered my life like a ray of sunshine on a gloomy day, like heat melting ice. I've got to tell you that I've always had a thing for blondes, especially brown-eyed blondes, and, sweetheart, you're more than any one man has a right to expect. A beautiful, brown-eyed blonde with dimples!"

Susan couldn't contain her smile. Thatch smiled in return, then said soberly, "All truthful compliments aside, this is serious business. I'm not sure I can adequately explain, but I know I have to try. In return, I expect you to stop your lies, too, and share yourself as willingly with me."

"Thatch, I don't—"

"Please, sweetheart," he murmured, "call me honey or something. Thatch is getting so repetitive. Anyway, yes, Thatch is part of my name, though actually…'' He lowered his voice, placed his mouth near her ear as he drew her closer, then began to tell her who he was and what he was doing on the ship.

Susan drew back in surprise, staring at him in both amazement and amusement as his story unraveled.

"So you see," he said casually, "I long ago took you off my list for anything other than wife material." He shrugged. "I'm not sure when I decided on that. Early on, but then I think spending day in and day out—not to mention night in and night out—with you has helped me get to know you more quickly than I would have in a conventional dating relationship."

"We haven't had a date!" she declared.

"Of course we have," he said. "I think the first one was the shopping expedition in Puerto Vallarta."

Susan grinned. "I suppose you're right. Good heavens! That seems so long ago."

He grinned. "Yes, it does. I feel as if I've known you all my life."

"Maybe it helps that you read a dossier on me," she said with a trace of ire. "What a sneaky thing to do."

He shrugged. "No slight intended. I read about everyone."

"And I was the only rich one, huh?" Susan said, the trace of ire in her voice growing.

He shook his head. "Sorry to disappoint you, sweetheart. Several of the passengers are richer than you."

Susan had to smile at that, too, but the smile quickly faded. "You know all about me, but now I'm not so sure what I know about you. You've been lying repeatedly to me."

"Only in the line of duty," he said seriously. "And, anyway, you haven't exactly kept away from your own little deceptions, and you can't even use the job as an excuse."

"You mean the rich thing," she said, glancing away from him.

He cupped her chin as they continued to dance. "I mean the rich thing. Stop running away from it. That's what you're doing, you know. That's why you're out here on this ship, isn't it?" He searched her eyes. "As your future husband, I need to know."

"I haven't agreed to marry you!" she cried so loudly that other people turned to look.

He squeezed her hand that sported the diamond. "You have. You just don't know it."

"I had the distinct impression that the rich weren't high on your list of favorite people," she said dryly. "And you know now that I'm very, very rich."

"I don't discriminate against *all* rich," he said, with a ghost of a grin. "Only those who insult me."

"And is that often?" she asked, looking into his blue eyes.

Thatch grinned self-mockingly. "Boy, this is bare-it-all time, isn't it?"

"I hope so, Thatch," she said sincerely. "I need to know all about you. I need to know that you aren't after my money."

"Why?" he asked bluntly. "You don't want your money. You're ashamed of it, aren't you?"

Susan lowered the brown eyes Thatch found so beautiful. "You wouldn't understand."

"Try me," he urged. "I need to know about this money hang-up you have."

Her eyes lifted. "It's not a hang-up," she said defensively.

Thatch gazed at her without saying anything, giving her time to think about what she'd said.

She sighed. "All right. It is." She searched his face. "Oh, Thatch, it's so complicated, and it goes back so far. You see, Mother married Father for his money so that she could have all the material things she wanted. Harriston was a good old Southern name, but her family fell on hard times after bad investments when Mother was twelve—a most vulnerable age. Suddenly she was ostracized from exclusive clubs, shunned by former friends. Gran rented out rooms in the mansion, creating an uproar in the exclusive neighborhood."

Thatch arched his brows. "I imagine that would do it."

"Oh, that wasn't all," Susan said. "They lost the house and had to move in with poor relatives." She twisted her hands together. "Mother never got over the shame or the lack of money. Money was—*is*—her sole obsession. She married my father only because he had money, and she wants me to marry some man just for his wealth. She says I owe it to her."

"How do you know she married your father for his money?" Thatch asked gently.

Susan looked surprised. "Everybody knows it."

"Who's everybody?" Thatch probed.

She shrugged and became embarrassed. She began to stroke her neck. "All the people I grew up around."

"Your father's only been dead a few years, hasn't he?" Thatch pressed.

Susan nodded.

"And your parents' marriage lasted twenty-plus years, didn't it?"

She nodded again.

"I know longevity doesn't mean love, but how do you feel? You were there. Do you think your parents loved each other?"

Wide brown eyes searched serious blue ones. "Why are you asking me such personal questions, Thatch?" Susan asked uncomfortably.

He met her gaze. "Because you need to ask yourself these questions, Susan. Stop running from your mother and stop judging and stop listening to other voices. Maybe your mother married for money—she apparently needed that very much—but maybe she married for love, too."

The color drained from Susan's face. "My father loved her," she said in a tiny voice. "He truly did." She nodded. "And, yes, in her own way, I believe my mother loved him. He did everything in his power to make her happy, and she appreciated that."

"Then that's all that matters," Thatch said. "Not what other people said about the marriage."

"That's not all that matters!" Susan insisted vehemently. "She's still trying to make me do what she did! She's subtly and not so subtly insisting that I owe it to her to make the 'proper' match, to marry into the moneyed circles. She still doesn't feel vindicated. She wants me to complete that for her."

Thatch shrugged as if it were the most inconsequential problem in the world. "That's your mother's problem. You're an adult. You don't owe your mother your future. Tell her no."

Thatch made it sound so simple, but after all the years Julia had ingrained social acceptance and Susan's ingratitude for her advantages, Susan didn't find it simple at all.

"You don't understand this kind of pressure," she said passionately.

"No?" he questioned. "Are you sure? I fell in love with a blonde who told me she could buy and sell me because she became angry when I wouldn't go to work for her father's multimillion-dollar business. It's all the same thing—blackmail in the name of love for someone's own interests. I just said no, thank you very much."

"It hurt, didn't it?" Susan asked, perceptively seeing the flicker of pain in Thatch's eyes.

Thatch almost went on the defensive, but they were sharing honesty. He realized that he needed this airing of old scars as badly as Susan did.

"It hurt like hell. But I'm still here," he said softly, "and so are you." He grinned. "Anyway, your problem solved itself. You're going to marry me, and that's that."

"Charles said you were after my money," Susan murmured.

Thatch chuckled. "No, thanks. You don't want it and I don't want it. Let your mother have it. Anyway, Charles doesn't know a thing about me. I don't want your money, Susan, but I think perhaps Charles might. He wants somebody's."

"He's not the thief," Susan said quickly.

"How do you know?" Thatch asked, frowning.

She shrugged. "Intuition, I guess. I don't think he would endanger his career."

At just that moment, Eva tapped Thatch on the shoulder. He was bent on ignoring all intruders until he saw who it was.

"Thatch," Eva whispered urgently, "you need to come with me right now!"

Instantly alert, he murmured to Susan, "Excuse me, and hold that last thought."

Susan wasn't sure what thought she was supposed to hold. She watched in surprise as Thatch discreetly vanished from the room, Eva going one way, Thatch the other. He hadn't told her anything about Eva Adkins.

When she saw Charles headed in her direction, Susan couldn't face him. She was in no mood to hear whatever he had to say. She had too much to think about. Escaping as quickly as Thatch, Susan made her way up to the Fiesta Deck.

She was startled when Charles pursued her. For a moment, she thought that it was Thatch returning, then she heard Charles's harsh voice.

"Susan, just what do you think you're doing?"

"About what?" she asked innocently. She had too many things on her mind to talk with Charles, especially until she knew the rest of Thatch's story and what Eva wanted with him.

"About what?" he all but spat. "About us! About being seen all over this ship with that—that con artist."

"He's not a con artist!" Susan defended hotly, then reminded herself to calm down. Now was no time to mess things up for Thatch, whatever he was doing.

Charles grasped her by the shoulders and forced her to look into his eyes. Susan tried to brush his hands off, but his fingers held firmly onto her flesh.

"You're a great disappointment to me, Susan," he growled. "I thought you were something special. I thought you were the woman I wanted to marry."

"The hell you say!" she shot back, using Thatch's favorite curse. "You think I'm rich and you're as relentless as my mother. You came from nothing and you want money, money, money! That's what you want. Well, once and for all, give up, Charles. I don't love you. I'm in love with Thatch and . . ."

Her words trailed off. She'd opened up to Thatch and now she couldn't seem to close up. She hadn't meant to tell Charles she was in love with Thatch.

He glared at her, then roughly released her. "I do want money," he declared. "I've never denied it. But I also want a woman with class. I've seen on this cruise that you don't have the qualities I want in a woman, Susan."

"Actually, that's a relief," Susan said honestly.

"You're a fool!" Charles said indignantly. "When Thatch—or whoever he is—is through with you, remember I'm the one who warned you, and I'm the one who says you deserve whatever you get. Now, if you'll excuse me, I'll go talk to the captain about your con artist."

Susan felt a moment of panic. Then she remembered that Thatch had told her the captain knew all about the investigation. Nothing would come of poor Charles's ranting. She sighed. At least he wouldn't rant at her anymore! She drew in a steadying breath

All the same, she couldn't help worrying about Thatch.

It was almost midnight when Thatch located her. Susan was frantic by then, a million worries running amok inside her head. She hadn't known what to do but wait on the dimly lit deck, staring out at the dark sea as the ship plowed through it, the New Year's Eve music echoing faintly in her ears.

"Thatch!" she cried when she saw him. "I didn't know what to think."

He grinned. "Think that I shouldn't have boasted so soon about being such a good private eye," he said, looking a bit worse for wear. "Eva solved the case, but poor Roger Nester put up a hell of a fight."

"Roger Nester?" Susan asked, stunned. "That nice little old man with the British accent? Why, he was on the last two cruises!"

"The one and the same," Thatch said. "He was high on my list," he added in self-defense, "but Eva spent so much time with him that she was fairly well convinced he wasn't the thief. Fortunately, or unfortunately, Roger was after Eva's pearls instead of her. She was alerted when she wore the pearls tonight and he noticed when he picked her up at her stateroom that the catch was loose."

"I remember her saying something about that at the first exercise class," Susan said. "Why didn't she have the clasp fixed? She could have had that done at the jewelry store."

Thatch grinned. "That's the way we caught the thief, sweetheart. The loose clasp was something we made up, just as we made up the origin of the pearls.

I bought them in L.A. for a few hundred dollars. An accomplished thief would have known that. Roger was just an impoverished soul with a phony title."

"Oh, the poor man," Susan murmured.

"The poor man?" Thatch repeated. "The poor man is a thief, making a lot of poor ladies terribly unhappy."

"Yes," Susan agreed. "That's certainly true, but he seemed so nice."

Thatch winked. "That's how he gets to his victims, and that's certainly not very nice, is it?"

"No, it isn't. I guess I just feel sorry for people who want money desperately enough to do such things."

"People like your mother who marry for money?" Thatch asked.

Susan shook her head, realizing that Thatch had lifted a terrible burden off her shoulders by making her question her beliefs about her mother. "I don't truly know that she did that, do I? And I do know Mother never stole anything! Speaking of which, I don't understand Laurent's part in the thefts. Charles caught him red-handed with a diamond necklace."

"Charles only thought he did," Thatch said. "Roger, in his ineptness, had put the necklace in an envelope designated for gratuities. He'd sealed it and left it in a conspicuous place in his cabin. When the alarm was sounded at the very end of the cruise about the missing necklace, Roger didn't have it, either. Laurent had thought the envelope was meant for him. When he'd discovered what was in it, and reported it, he couldn't recall which cabin it had come from."

"And Charles took credit for catching the thief!" Susan said in disbelief.

"Yes, I'm afraid he wanted a star in his career crown," Thatch said dryly. "Laurent agreed to work with management until we could find the real thief."

"And Eva works with you," Susan said.

Thatch nodded. "Roger, who's been living off stolen jewels, made a mistake in her case. He picked the wrong woman. He told Eva she should leave her pearls in the room, then he made a pretense of needing her key to go back and get something that had fallen from his pocket. It was so obvious what he was going to do. We caught him right in the act."

"Money again," Susan said, "or the lack of it. Look at all the people he's involved and upset. A cruise should be the vacation of a lifetime."

"Say, speaking of that," Thatch said, "you were right—I've had the best time of my life on the cruise, and now I want it to last forever. I want *us* to last forever. You did say you would marry me, didn't you?"

"You mean, you want to marry a poor girl like me?" she teased, her heart hammering madly. Thatch had said he wanted *forever* with her!

"Oh, are you suddenly poor?" he asked, smiling. "Did someone steal your textile mills in my absence?"

She nodded. "Something like that. You know, I think you're very wise, Daniel Thatcher Thomas."

"Oh, please do call me Thatch now," he said. "I'm beginning to like the way you say it, and you know I told you that's what my friends call me." He winked at her. "We are friends, aren't we?"

"Yes, Thatch," she said with a dazzling smile, "we're friends, and yes, I'll marry you and spend forever with you; however, I'm trying to tell you I'm *re-*

ally going to be poor. I'm going to give the money to Mother, as you suggested, and I'm also going to quit sailing the seas. Though I do love it, it's an escape I no longer need."

"I see," he said, pensively tugging on his beard. "Actually, that's too bad. I was beginning to like ocean travel. I'd just about decided to give up being a private eye. You were right about that. I've gotten too jaded. I've begun to see only the negative side of people. Until you."

He pulled her into his arms and bent his head to kiss her.

Susan pressed her palms against his shoulders. "Now wait a minute, mister! You're supposed to be the practical one," she said. "What will we do if we both give up money and work?"

He shrugged. "Oh, we'll think of something. For the coming week, we'll live off love. Then we'll get married in Los Angeles."

"And then?" she prompted.

He seemed thoroughly perplexed as he tugged distractedly on his beard. "And then I'll shave this thing off," he said, grinning at her.

"Thatch, be serious!" she cried. "What about the future?"

"Oh, that," he said. "Well, let's see, since you like sailing and I like sailing, maybe we'll just saunter down to the seaside and get ourselves a small boat. I'm really getting into the romance aspect of cruise travel. We could take people to sea on a real small operation—say for two or three days." He snapped his fingers. "And we could further cut expenses by living on the boat."

Susan's brown eyes were wide. "Are you being serious?" she asked.

Thatch chuckled. "If it interests you at all, I am. I've got a few dollars put aside. We might have to figure out how to pay at least one good sailor to help us, but I kind of find the idea appealing. How about you?"

She looked deeply into his eyes, and saw her own reflection glowing there. "I think it's a wonderful idea. I really do love the sea and being with people." She winked at him. "We'd be partners, right?"

"Yes, of course," he agreed.

She smiled. "Then I'll have to contribute a little something to the cost of the venture myself, say a hundred thousand, or so."

"Oh, no!" he said. "No way. That's not fair. I can't match that much," he protested. "I said a small operation."

Susan laughed. "Everything's relative, remember? A hundred thousand is nothing to a rich lady, so all things being equal, my share is fair for me, while I still have it."

"Susan—"

"Now, don't let your ego get in the way of our future," she insisted. "Besides," she said with another wink, "I'm a liberated woman. We'll figure something out to make it seem fairer—a trade of some sort."

Thatch chuckled. "You're incorrigible, Susan Williams."

"Not yet," she said, smiling. "But I'm working on it."

She wrapped her arms around Thatch and drew him toward her. "Beginning right this minute," she said, accepting the kiss he'd started to give her minutes earlier—a kiss worthy of forever!

*   *   *   *   *

COMING NEXT MONTH

#820 PILLOW TALK—Patricia Ellis
Written in the Stars
Kendall Arden had made a big mistake in getting involved with
Jared Dalton's research on sleep. How could she confess her sensual
dreams to this oh-so-dedicated Libra man? Especially since he was the
subject of her fantasies....

#821 AND DADDY MAKES THREE—Anne Peters
Eric Schwenker firmly believed that a mother's place was at home, so why
was Isabel Mott using *his* office to care for her daughter? Maybe Isabel
could teach him about working mothers . . . and what a family truly was.

#822 CASEY'S FLYBOY—Vivian Leiber
Cautious Casey Stevens knew what she wanted—a decent, *civilized* home
for her baby. But sexy flyboy Leon Brodie tempted her to spread her wings
and fly. The handsome pilot was a good reason to let herself soar....

#823 PAPER MARRIAGE—Judith Bowen
Justine O'Malley was shocked by rancher Clayton Truscott's marriage
proposal—but then, so was he. Clayton had sworn never to trust a woman
again. But to keep his brother's children, he would do anything—
even *marry!*

#824 BELOVED STRANGER—Peggy Webb
Belinda Stubaker was incensed! Her employer, Reeve Lawrence, was
acting like Henry Higgins—insisting on teaching her the finer things in
life. How could Belinda explain to Reeve that *love* was the finest thing
there was....

#825 HOME FOR THANKSGIVING—Suzanne Carey
One kiss, so many years ago. Now, Dr. Aaron Dash and Kendra Jenkins
were colleagues at the same hospital. But that kiss could never be
forgotten. Beneath their professionalism, an intense passion
still lingered....

AVAILABLE THIS MONTH:

#814 THROUGH MY EYES
Helen R. Myers

#815 MAN TROUBLE
Marie Ferrarella

#816 DANCE UNTIL DAWN
Brenda Trent

#817 HOMETOWN HERO
Kristina Logan

#818 PATCHWORK FAMILY
Carla Cassidy

#819 EVAN
Diana Palmer

WRITTEN IN THE STARS

MAN OF
HER DREAMS?

Will sexy Libra Jared Dalton make Kendall
Arden's dreams come true? Find out in
Patricia Ellis's PILLOW TALK, October's
WRITTEN IN THE STARS book!

Kendall didn't know what she was letting
herself in for when she agreed to help the
perfect Libra with his psychology project.
Jared's every glance awoke feelings she'd
never before experienced—and promised to
fulfill *all* her fantasies: . . .

PILLOW TALK by Patricia Ellis . . . only
from Silhouette Romance in October. It's
WRITTEN IN THE STARS!

Available in October at your favorite retail outlet, or order your copy now by sending your name
address, zip or postal code, along with a check or money order for $2.59 (please do not sen
cash), plus 75¢ postage and handling ($1.00 in Canada) for each book ordered, payable t
Silhouette Reader Service to:

In the U.S.

3010 Walden Avenue
P.O. Box 1396
Buffalo, NY 14269-1396

In Canada

P.O. Box 609
Fort Erie, Ontario
L2A 5X3

Please specify book title with your order.
Canadian residents add applicable federal and provincial taxes.

OCTSTA

Silhouette Romance®

SILHOUETTE®
OFFICIAL SWEEPSTAKES
RULES

NO PURCHASE NECESSARY

To enter, complete an Official Entry Form or 3" × 5" index card by hand-printing, in plain block letters, your complete name, address, phone number and age, and mailing it to: Silhouette Fashion A Whole New You Sweepstakes, P.O. Box 9056, Buffalo, NY 14269-9056.

No responsibility is assumed for lost, late or misdirected mail. Entries must be sent separately with first class postage affixed, and be received no later than December 31, 1991 for eligibility.

Winners will be selected by D.L. Blair, Inc., an independent judging organization whose decisions are final, in random drawings to be held on January 30, 1992 in Blair, NE at 10:00 a.m. from among all eligible entries received.

The prizes to be awarded and their approximate retail values are as follows: Grand Prize — A brand-new Ford Explorer 4×4 plus a trip for two (2) to Hawaii, including round-trip air transportation, six (6) nights hotel accommodation, a $1,400 meal/spending money stipend and $2,000 cash toward a new fashion wardrobe (approximate value: $28,000) or $15,000 cash; two (2) Second Prizes — A trip to Hawaii, including round-trip air transportation, six (6) nights hotel accommodation, a $1,400 meal/spending money stipend and $2,000 cash toward a new fashion wardrobe (approximate value: $11,000) or $5,000 cash; three (3) Third Prizes — $2,000 cash toward a new fashion wardrobe. All prizes are valued in U.S. currency. Travel award air transportation is from the commercial airport nearest winner's home. Travel is subject to space and accommodation availability, and must be completed by June 30, 1993. Sweepstakes offer is open to residents of the U.S. and Canada who are 21 years of age or older as of December 31, 1991, except residents of Puerto Rico, employees and immediate family members of Torstar Corp., its affiliates, subsidiaries, and all agencies, entities and persons connected with the use, marketing, or conduct of this sweepstakes. All federal, state, provincial, municipal and local laws apply. Offer void wherever prohibited by law. Taxes and/or duties, applicable registration and licensing fees, are the sole responsibility of the winners. Any litigation within the province of Quebec respecting the conduct and awarding of a prize may be submitted to the Régie des loteries et courses du Québec. All prizes will be awarded; winners will be notified by mail. No substitution of prizes is permitted.

Potential winners must sign and return any required Affidavit of Eligibility/Release of Liability within 30 days of notification. In the event of noncompliance within this time period, the prize may be awarded to an alternate winner. Any prize or prize notification returned as undeliverable may result in the awarding of that prize to an alternate winner. By acceptance of their prize, winners consent to use of their names, photographs and/or their likenesses for purposes of advertising, trade and promotion on behalf of Torstar Corp. without further compensation. Canadian winners must correctly answer a time-limited arithmetical question in order to be awarded a prize.

For a list of winners (available after 3/31/92), send a separate stamped, self-addressed envelope to: Silhouette Fashion A Whole New You Sweepstakes, P.O. Box 4665, Blair, NE 68009.

PREMIUM OFFER TERMS

receive your gift, complete the Offer Certificate according to directions. Be certain to enclose the required number of "Fashion A Whole New You" proofs of product purchase (which are found on the last page of every specially marked "Fashion A Whole New You" Silhouette or Harlequin romance novel). Requests must be received later than December 31, 1991. Limit: four (4) gifts per name, family, group, organization or address. Items depicted are for illustrative purposes only and may not be exactly as shown. Please allow 6 to 8 weeks for receipt of order. Offer good while quantities of gifts last. In the event an ordered gift is no longer available, you will receive a free, previously unpublished Silhouette or Harlequin book for every proof of purchase you have submitted with your request, plus a refund of the postage and handling charge you have included. Offer good in the U.S. and Canada only.

SLFW·SWPR

SILHOUETTE® OFFICIAL SWEEPSTAKES ENTRY FORM

4-FWSRS-2

Complete and return this Entry Form immediately – the mo₤ entries you submit, the better your chances of winning!

- Entries must be received by **December 31, 1991.**
- A Random draw will take place on **January 30, 1992.**
- No purchase necessary.

Yes, I want to win a FASHION A WHOLE NEW YOU Sensuous and Adventurous prize from Silhouette

Name _____ Telephone _____ Age ____

Address _____

City _____ State _____ Zip _____

Return Entries to: Silhouette **FASHION A WHOLE NEW YOU,**
P.O. Box 9056, Buffalo, NY 14269-9056   © 1991 Harlequin Enterprises Limite

PREMIUM OFFER

To receive your free gift, send us the required number of proofs-of-purchase from any speciall marked FASHION A WHOLE NEW YOU Silhouette or Harlequin Book with the Offer Certificat₤ properly completed, plus a check or money order (do not send cash) to cover postage and handlin₤ payable to Silhouette FASHION A WHOLE NEW YOU Offer. We will send you the specified gif₤

OFFER CERTIFICATE

Item	A. SENSUAL DESIGNER VANITY BOX COLLECTION (set of 4) (Suggested Retail Price $60.00)	B. ADVENTUROUS TRAVEL COSMETI₤ CASE SET (set of 3) (Suggested Retail Price $25.00)
# of proofs-of-purchase	18	12
Postage and Handling	$3.50	$2.95
Check one	☐	☐

Neme _____

Address _____

City _____ State _____ Zip _____

Mail this certificate, designated number of proofs-of-purchase and check or money order f₤ postage and handling to: Silhouette **FASHION A WHOLE NEW YOU Gift Offer,** P.O. Box 905₤ Buffalo, NY 14269-9057. Requests must be received by December 31, 1991.

ONE PROOF-OF-PURCHASE

4-FWSRP-2

To collect your fabulous free gift you must include the necessary number of proofs-of-purchase with a properly completed Offer Certificate.

© 1991 Harlequin Enterprises Limited

See previous page for details.